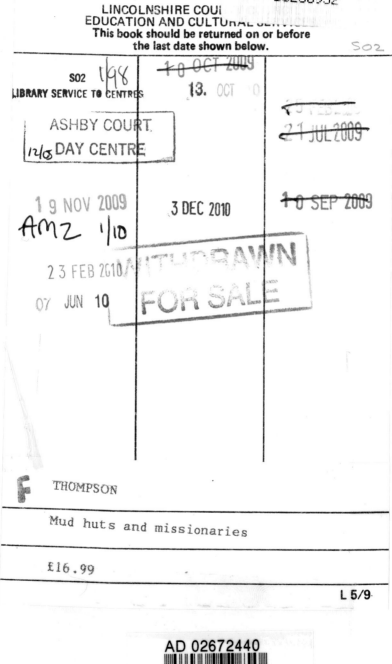

MUD HUTS AND MISSIONARIES

Recent Titles by E. V. Thompson

MUD HUTS AND MISSIONARIES

E V Thompson

This first world edition published in Great Britain 1997 by
SEVERN HOUSE PUBLISHERS LTD of
9–15 High Street, Sutton, Surrey SM1 1DF.
This title first published in the U.S.A.1998 by
SEVERN HOUSE PUBLISHERS INC of
595 Madison Avenue, New York, N.Y. 10022.

British Library Cataloguing in Publication Data

Thompson, E. V.
    Mud huts and missionaries
    1.   Africa - Fiction
    1.   Title
    823.9'14 [F]

ISBN 0-7278-5289-2 [cased]
ISBN 0-7278-7015-7 [paper]

Typeset by Hewer Text Composition Services Ltd,
Edinburgh, Scotland.
Printed and bound in Great Britain by
MPG Books Ltd, Bodmin, Cornwall

Contents

Introduction

THIS is a collection of short stories that is not only of the past, but also *from* the past. They are stories of an Africa that is no more. For some who were once the favoured few, its passing is a matter of regret and, perhaps, resentment.

I lived in Africa during a time which was regarded by the few as the twilight of all that was best in the history of this great and remarkable continent.

For the vast majority of its peoples, its demise heralded the casting off of shackles. The shackles of colonialism. It was a new dawn. The sun was rising on their dreams and aspirations. They would stretch out their arms and reach into the modern world. When they had it in their grasp, many preferred to forget all that had gone before. The good and the bad. It was the Africa of the old men and women. Today was for the *new* African.

In the cities, the new Africa was being shaped on the anvils of politics and ambition. In the more remote villages, even in the days when I lived there, life was lived in much the same way as it had been for very many years.

The people were not simple, but they lived simplistic lives. They realised that the world about them was

1

changing, yet they clung to what was familiar, for as long as was possible.

I was delighted to learn that this collection will now be available in its native setting. A number of these stories were published or broadcast in that, the 'old' Africa. They are fictional, but they are based on much that I learned in Africa. Inspired by the wealth of legend which exists in connection with the animals, birds and plants who have their homes on that vast continent, some have been told around the camp-fires of various tribes for countless generations – but most of the stories are new. They owe their origin to my imagination and tell of the beginnings of some of the lesser known creatures in the way I would like things to have happened – and who knows? I could even be correct!

The other stories tell of those who came from the villages. Their way of life has vanished forever. Perhaps it never was . . . ? It will certainly never return. Neither the mud huts, nor the missionaries . . .

E V Thompson, 1997

Njiri's Tail

MANY, many seasons ago, so many that even the giant balancing rocks were young, the trees would nod their heads to the wind and bid it "Good Morning" and the wind would pause to speak of all the things it had seen during its journey from the rising sun.

While the wise wind spoke, the animals and Man would seat themselves in a circle on the ground and listen, occasionally uttering polite words of wonder or nodding sagely when the wind mentioned something that they knew about.

For in those days, you see, Man, the animals, the trees and the wind spoke with one tongue and lived in peace, each having no fear of the other.

That is the way it was and had been ever since time began, but recently the wind had been bringing them very disturbing news. He told of the tribes far to the North who quarrelled bitterly with each other. They had made long sticks with sharp, shiny iron ends, which they called spears, and which they used to kill each other and the animals who had been their friends for so long.

So bad were these people now that they killed the animals for no other reason than to obtain fur with which to decorate their bodies and their spears and to provide hides with which they made shields to protect themselves from the spears of their enemies.

Even now, said the wind, these tribes were advancing down through the country, spreading fear ahead of them. No one had been able to withstand them because the people of this country were peaceful and had no knowledge of fighting. They knew only how to till the land and gather their crops.

Njiri, the wart-hog, and Man were talking about it as they stood by the great river watching the hippopotamus cooling his huge body and yawning cavernously to expose peg-like teeth.

Man was very unhappy. "Perhaps," he said, "they will not wish to come so far, or, if they do, they may look upon the width of the great river and return to their homes."

Njiri shook his head, sadly. "No. The wise wind has told us how these tribes cut down the trees and by using our friend, fire, burn out a space inside the trees into which they climb and travel upon the water, even, said the wind, upon the great lakes of the North. No, they will not be stopped by the river."

Man said no more but sunk into a gloomy silence which upset Njiri because he was very fond of his friend. But try as he might, he could think of no way in which he could help him.

The next morning the wind arrived in a great hurry. So great, that his passing disturbed the surface of the great river and bowed the reeds until their heads were touching the water. As he sped onto the land he told his story to the trees and they groaned and writhed in agitation.

Finally, he came to the place where Man and the animals were seated. "They are here," he cried. "The tribes are here. Even now they sit on the far bank of the river sharpening their spears and hollowing out the trees for the river crossing."

Man and the animals looked at each other fearfully. Of them all man was frightened the most because the wind had told how these tribes drove man from his home, killing him if he did not flee before them. "Oh! What are we to do?" he wailed.

"Wind," said Njiri, "what does this thing they call a spear look like?"

"Come with me, Njiri," replied the wind. "I brought one with me across the great river. It floats now in the reeds by the bank."

The wind swirled away and Njiri ran after him, as fast as his short, sturdy legs would carry him.

5

At the water's edge the wind stopped and gently parted the reeds and there, floating among them, was the spear. At one end it had a shiny blade, broad and sharp and with a wicked-looking point. A brown, polished stick was fixed to the blade, the other end of the stick being adorned with a tuft of monkey fur.

Njiri looked at the spear and shuddered. "This, then, is the thing with which these tribes kill each other?"

"Yes," hissed the wind. "With this in their hand nothing is safe from them."

Njiri looked again at the thing in the water, bobbing up and down with the wind's anger. He looked first at the monkey fur at one end, then at the handle

6

and the broad blade, and back again to the monkey fur.

Turning his head he peered behind him, to where his long tail, with the tuft of coarse hair, hung. He had an idea! But to carry it out he would require the assistance of the wind.

"Wind," he said, "I think I know how we can stop these tribes from coming into our land and destroying all we have."

Quickly he told of his plan and the wind became so excited that he whirled around and shot up into the air, carrying leaves and sticks with him.

"Njiri," he said, when he came down again, "you may have a face that makes all who see it want to smile, but you have a very clever brain. Yes, I will help you. Go now and find all your brothers. I will wait in the middle of the river for the coming of the tribes."

Off he went, with a "Wheeeeee!" of excitement, while Njiri hurried away to gather his very large family and explain his plan to them.

So it was that, very soon, there were hundreds of wart-hogs hidden near the path that ran alongside the river, unseen from the water because of the reeds. They waited and waited until suddenly there came to them the voice of the wind, shrill and loud. "They come, they come! Quickly, Njiri, they come."

At the signal, Njiri and his family ran out onto the path with their tails held high in the air. Backwards and forwards behind the reeds they ran, their feet making a thunderous din on the hard ground.

From the river they could hear the cries of fear from those in the boats. They heard them shout to those who

7

were behind them to turn around quickly. So terrified were they that some of the boats overturned, tipping their occupants into the river. With much panic they all fled back to the far bank and once there did not stop running until the river was far behind them.

You see, when Njiri and his family started running to and fro behind the reeds, all that could be seen from the river were the ends of their upright tails, and each one looked exactly like the end of a spear with the monkey fur fixed to it. The tribes received such a surprise at the thought of so many warriors ready to fight them that they never returned again.

So it was that Njiri, the wart-hog, saved Man and all the other animals.

All this happened many years ago and man and the other animals have long since forgotten about it – but the wart-hog still remembers. If you do not believe me, then the very next time you see a wart-hog, you watch him very closely. When the wind, blowing from the river, reaches him and whispers in his ear that the tribes are coming, you will see his long tail, with the tuft on the end, go straight up into the air and he will start trotting along, exactly as he did on that day, far away in the long ago.

The Hunter

IT was late March. A warm, pleasant evening, with rains a recent memory and the crops safely gathered in. The men of the village, bellies comfortably full and pipes crackling contentedly, sat around the fire in the carefully swept space before the hut of the headman.

The transient reflection of the flames touched briefly upon dark skins. Some were smooth and shiny, others creased and wrinkled with the wisdom and humour of age.

This was the daily meeting place of the men. They came when the sunset, with its attendant train of vivid colours, had faded and the moon and stars had replaced it with a softer light. For hour after hour they would talk and reminisce, shutting out the sounds of the African night as it closed in around them.

Tonight they had been listening to the exploits of Pasipamire. He had recently returned from a safari, on which he had been accompanying a party of American tourists.

When he had left the village some two months before, it was said he had been hired as a kitchen-hand. Tonight, the villagers learned differently. It seemed he had been

9

gun-bearer, tracker and hunter and generally indispensable to the whole safari.

Now, as the fire burned low, Chigavara, the old headman, spoke.

"Tongesayi, it is almost time for the older ones among us to seek the shelter of our huts and the comfort of our blankets. Send us away happy, with one of your stories."

The suggestion was taken up by the others. Tongesayi was a popular storyteller.

"Yes, let us have a story."

"Give us a tale that will be a suitable end to a day that has been kind to us."

Removing the pipe from his mouth, Tongesayi cleared his throat and spat accurately into the heart of the dying fire.

Locking skinny arms about bony knees, he rocked backwards and forwards thoughtfully for a few minutes. Then his lips opened in a toothless smile. His voice, when he spoke, belied his great age. It was clear and strong, like a boy's.

"Yes, I have a story for you. One that is true, as some of you may remember, and it is not without mirth. It tells of Mandi, who lived in this very village. He was a good hunter. No, a *mighty* hunter, as he was fond of telling all who could be persuaded to listen to him.

"If Mandi returned from the hunt with only a dove for the pot, he would tell you of the wild pig which had slipped through his grasp. A small buck slung over his shoulder would bring forth a tale of the lion he had fought for an hour before the king of beasts conceded ownership of the buck to Mandi.

The Hunter

"The incident I will now relate, occurred here, on this very spot where we are now seated. It was just such a night as this, with the warriors of the tribe telling the stories our people have told for many years. I was seated well back from the fire – I was a very young man then.

"Now, in those days, lions were even more troublesome than they are today. Especially those which had taken to feeding upon the flesh of man. Two such animals were known to be in the area around the village. Hunting parties went out against them, but they could not be tracked down. What was worse, each party would return with one man missing and no one able to say how, or when, he disappeared.

"The warriors were completely at a loss as to the best method of catching these maneaters – but not Mandi. In a very loud voice, he was telling the others how *he* would deal with the mighty beasts. Suddenly, from the edge of the village, just beyond the last house, there came the roar of a hungry lion.

"There was the briefest murmur of time in which no man moved. Then, as though a magic wind had blown through the village, there was not a man left sitting beside the fire.

"The stealthy steps of the lion padded across the clearing near the fire and the beast sneezed as the dust raised by so many rapidly departing men began to settle.

"From the hut where Mandi and seven other men had sought refuge, there was the sound of chattering teeth and heavy breathing. Then a tremulous voice whispered, 'Oh Mandi, great hunter. Go out from this hut and rid us of this hungry lion.'

11

" 'Ah! If only I could,' replied Mandi. 'But my hunting spear is standing in the corner of my own hut.'

" 'Then you may take mine,' came the voice of the owner of the hut in which they were sheltering. 'Here. It is good and stout and should suffice, even for such a hunter as yourself.'

"There was a brief silence before Mandi spoke again. 'I thank you. It is a very good friend indeed who would loan another man his best hunting spear, but I fear I am unable to accept your noble offer. Such is my strength that I have been known to break the strongest spear, and I know what a man's spear means to him.'

"There were many derisive remarks and rude noises from the other occupants of the hut before the owner spoke once again. 'If this is all that is stopping you, then you need worry no more. I make you a present of the spear. What warrior would not risk his *own* spear for the sake of his neighbours?'

"Mandi knew he now had no choice but to leave the hut and hunt the lion. To refuse would brand him as a coward for ever. In view of his previous boasting, he would become a laughing stock for even the smallest of boys.

"Clutching his unwelcome present in a trembling hand, Mandi slowly opened the door of the hut. He hoped with all his heart that by now the lion would have left the village to seek its evening meal elsewhere.

"Leaving the door standing wide open behind him, he took a first, careful step outside. For more than a minute he stood quietly, eyes rolling white in his head as he sought that which he hoped he might not see.

"Suddenly, from not more than fifteen paces away, he

12

heard a low warning growl. There was the lion, crouching for the charge!

"A moment later, the beast charged forward and leaped at him. His legs suddenly weak, Mandi dropped to the ground in terror at the very last moment.

"The lion jumped right over him and its charge took it through the open doorway of the hut!

"Although Mandi was perhaps not the great hunter he claimed to be, there can be no doubt he could think more quickly than any man in the village. Scrambling to his feet, he slammed shut the door of the hut. In a voice that was heard in every house in the village, he shouted, 'There! I have caught him now. You men make sure he does not escape, while I go to seek his mate'."

The story was ended. It had been another happy evening. The men rose from the fire, chuckling happily at Tongesayi's story.

All except Pasipamire.

He looked at no one as he made his way to his own hut. When a lion roared in the far distance he jumped nervously and walked just a little faster.

Early To Rise

IN the quiet of the grey early dawn, old Chikwereti sat on a large flat rock, beneath an ancient msasa tree. A blanket was pulled tightly about his shoulders and he sucked contentedly at his pipe.

This was the happiest hour of his day. A time when he was able to think about life as he had lived it. As it had been in those far off, quieter years.

Today, especially, he needed this brief period of peace. This was the day his grandson, Josaya, was coming to visit the family. It was to be a long stay. A month, the letter had stated.

Chikwereti groaned. Josaya had been home only three times during the last five years. On each occasion the whole of the day had been taken up in listening to the wonderful things he had done, and the grand life he led in the city. All told by Josaya himself, of course.

The old man sucked deeply on his pipe. Pulling a wry face, he coughed and spat over the edge of the rock. His pipe had gone out. Behind him he heard the long, first wail of a waking baby and the shrill, scolding voice of one of his many granddaughters. The village was awakening.

Tapping out the ashes from his pipe against the rock, Chikwereti stood up slowly. Painfully straightening out his stiff legs, he made his way to the hut he shared with the youngest of his daughters.

Josaya duly arrived and Chikwereti found him even less bearable than usual. He had received promotion in his employment and had the most beautiful girlfriend in the whole of the city. He had also acquired a bicycle; a transistor radio; a record-player . . . The list was endless. It brought forth gasps of delight from the women and silent, envious glances from the men.

Chikwereti alone remained unimpressed.

Only once did Josaya speak directly to him. It was when he described a shirt he possessed, which he claimed to be the colour of the summer sky.

"Something to delight the eyes of any woman," the old man commented. "Tell me, what gifts have you brought home for your mother?"

Chikwereti was not included in any more of Josaya's conversation that day. In spite of the stories of wealth he possessed in the city, Josaya had not brought home a present for his mother.

The following day, when the sun had almost reached its noonday peak, Chikwereti was seated in the shade of his hut. He idly watched a flock of cranes circling and wheeling high above the valley. Suddenly, he heard the sound of voices raised in excitement. They came from the direction of the fields beside the river.

At first, he ignored the noise. There were many snakes close to the water. The women had probably seen one of them. Then he recognised the voice of Josaya raised above all the others.

The voices drew closer and Chikwereti could hear

something of what was being said. One word was repeated over and over again. That word was . . . *gold*!

Very soon, a crowd of chattering villagers headed by Josaya stood before the old man. In his hand Josaya held a rock about the size of a man's thumbnail and he thrust it forward.

"Look, Chikwereti," he cried. "Look at what I have found in your field. In the place where my mother was working. It is gold, Chikwereti. Gold!"

He turned towards the crowd and held the rock above his head. "Look at this. Here in my hand is enough gold to buy beer for the men of the village for a whole year. There must be much more there."

He turned to face his grandfather once more. "With this I will become rich. One of the richest men in the whole of the land."

Chikwereti looked with contempt at the greed that shone from the other man's face. "Josaya," he said quietly. "I am not yet dead. The land from which that stone came is *my* land. If anyone becomes rich, it will be me. It could also be that I do not wish the gold to be taken from the ground."

Josaya's expression became one of cunning. "You can do nothing to prevent it, Chikwereti. Oh yes, you own the land, but you do not own the mineral rights. The gold can be mined by whoever makes a claim to it."

He paused, smirking at the old man. "I see you do not believe me. You will when the District Commissioner arrives. I, Josaya, am not one to waste time. Already someone is running to tell him of my discovery."

The District Commissioner arrived some two hours later and confirmed all that Josaya had said.

Chikwereti could not understand it. "But, this is *my* land," he protested. "It has always been mine. Am I not able to prevent other people from stealing that which is mine? Does this mean that strangers with their noisy engines and machines will come and tear up the ground where my crops are growing and I will be able to do nothing to stop them?"

The District Commissioner looked distinctly uncomfortable. "I am afraid so, Chikwereti," he said. "Of course, if a mining company takes over the operation you will be handsomely compensated for the damage they cause to your land."

The old man gave him a bitter look. "What can I be given that will mean more to me than watching my crops growing in the sunshine? I am an old man. To give me money is to throw a bone to a dog who no longer has teeth."

"I am sorry, Chikwereti, deeply sorry," the District Commissioner apologised, "but such matters do not rest in my hands. Josaya found the gold. He is quite entitled to register a claim for it." Examining the rock which Josaya had given to him, he said, "I am no expert, but I would say this is a very valuable find."

Placing the rock inside a small, canvas bag, he handed it to the jubilant young man, saying, "Take care of this, Josaya. In the morning I will send a vehicle to take you and your discovery to the Mines Department Assay Office. I suggest you keep this inside your hut for safety. It is worth a lot of money."

When the bag had been placed inside his hut for safe-keeping and the District Commissioner had gone, Josaya cast a sidelong glance of triumph in his grandfather's direction. Then he left to join the other men around the fire. Far into the night they would discuss ways of spending the money the gold was going to bring.

Chikwereti went inside his own hut early. He had no wish to speak to anyone, or have anyone speak to him.

He sat, an old and lonely figure until the sounds outside gradually died away. All the time he tried not to think of the small piece of rock that had the power to destroy the way of life he so loved.

As the fires burned low and the villagers slept, Chikwereti thought of the changes that must inevitably result from the discovery of gold on his land.

No more would he enjoy his hour of peace each morning, waiting for the sunrise. Throughout the day and night there would be dull explosions, the clattering of machinery and the constant hammer and thud of the stamp mills.

Chikwereti knew this because, many years before, he had visited a friend who worked on a gold mine.

The very landmarks would disappear. Hills would be flattened, the river diverted, and men would scurry in and out of the ground like ants.

All this would come to pass because Josaya had found the piece of rock that was in the small canvas bag.

No one knew how long Chikwereti remained awake with his thoughts, or even if he slept at all. When dawn came, it found him seated on the rock beneath the msasa tree. He was still there when the vehicle sent by the District Commissioner arrived.

Clutching the canvas bag and accompanied by two of his cousins, Josaya climbed inside the vehicle. It set off, bumping and jolting its way along the track, sent on its way by the waving hands of friends and relatives. The shouts of small boys pursued it until it gathered sufficient speed to leave them behind.

For two days there was an excited undercurrent of expectancy in the village, as they awaited news of Josaya and his gold-bearing rock.

On the third day, the two cousins returned, subdued and sullen. Josaya was not with them.

At first, they refused to say anything. But they could not hold out for ever against the intense curiosity of the whole village. Eventually, the story came out.

When they reached the assay office, the necessary tests were quickly carried out. Josaya's 'valuable' rock was found to contain a high percentage of iron pyrites. 'Fool's gold'. Nothing else.

"It is very fitting," declared Chikwereti, who come forward to stand at the edge of the crowd surrounding the two cousins. "Fool's gold. Gold for those who spend it before they know what it is worth. It is even more fitting that it should have been Josaya who discovered it. Now you will listen to me!"

He straightened up and for a few moments it was possible to see the man he had been many years before.

"You!" He stabbed a finger at Josaya's mother. "You will go to the place where this rock was found and pile it high with all the rocks and rubbish from the other plots of land. Never again will that piece of land be dug while I am alive. Otherwise another fool is likely to come along and find his 'gold' and once again upset the life of our village."

Accompanied by some of her relatives, Josaya's mother went off to carry out Chikwereti's orders.

Even before she was out of sight the villagers had forgotten their disappointment at the bad news brought by Josaya's cousins. Soon they were roaring with laughter at the mistake that had been made. The word 'fool' became synonymous with 'Josaya'.

Leaving them to their laughter, Chikwereti walked slowly to his tree-shaded rock. He was contentedly puffing at his pipe when the District Commissioner drove in to the village.

Leaving his vehicle, the District Commissioner walked over to the rock. He seated himself beside the old man, saying nothing until he too had lit his pipe.

Thoughtfully looking out across the land that sloped gently away from them, he said, "It's a lovely view from here, Chikwereti."

The old man nodded his agreement without looking at his companion.

"No danger of it being spoiled now, either," the District Commissioner continued. "Josaya has been made to appear such an idiot, I doubt if he'll ever be inclined to return and look for more gold."

Still Chikwereti said nothing.

"A pity, really." The District Commissioner shook spittle from his pipe stem. "It would have brought a great deal of prosperity to this part of the country."

The old man's eyes smouldered into life. With an expansive gesture he indicated the whole length of the valley that lay before them.

"Look! There is land. Good, rich land that will grow any crop. On the other side of the river you see strong, fat

20

cattle. They belong to my people. Is that not prosperity enough for anyone?"

The District Commissioner shrugged his shoulders. "Some people might not think so."

"Then let those people keep their thoughts to themselves until I am gone," Chikwereti retorted. "They will not have too long to wait. Until that time, this valley – my valley – will remain as I have always known it."

The District Commissioner rose to his feet and looked down at the old man. "This is exactly what I expected you to say, Chikwereti. I believe you are wrong. You cannot hold up progress for ever, you know. However, as you say, your people will have to wait. I will say nothing of what I know until it is time."

The District Commissioner made a great show of knocking out his pipe and filling it with tobacco once more. "Just for the record, how did you do it? How did you manage to exchange the rock I examined here for the one that Josaya took to the assay office? I know it must have been exchanged. Limited though my knowledge is, I *do* know the difference between gold and iron pyrites."

Chikwereti smiled, "It was not hard to do. I simply followed the habit of a lifetime. Many times I have told my children and grandchildren that to achieve anything in life they must rise early and set about the things that need to be done. This is what I did. While they were still sleeping I took the piece of gold from the sack and threw it in the river. I replaced it with a piece of fool's gold from the rocks behind the village."

He grinned. It was a toothless, happy expression that creased his face like the hide on an elephant's trunk, "You see, I too know the difference between fool's gold and

21

real gold. I found the real gold many, many years ago. I sat on this very spot and wondered what I should do. I sat here until the sky in the east was painted by the sun. I realised then where my people would find the gold that would keep them happy."

As he walked back to his vehicle, the District Commissioner paused to listen to the women singing in the fields as they worked. Change had to come, no one could hold back the progress that was advancing through the country. But for now . . .? They would need to rise early if they wanted to bring change to Chikwereti's lands.

iGola, The Cat

MAN was sitting in his comfortable cave. The fire just outside the entrance was burning brightly, its flames dancing up from the crackling wood casting moving shadows across the walls and lighting up the serious faces of the animals who were sitting listening to what Man was saying.

"We have been friends for a very long time," he said. "Ever since the first day, we have helped each other as best we could. On cold nights you often came here and shared my fire with me. When there was anything wrong with your families you brought them to me and I cured them. But I have decided that I too would like to find a mate for myself and so I must go far away, to where there are more people like myself. All this time I have thought that I was the only man, but the other day I met one the same as myself and he told me that far away there is a place where men live together, as many as there are animals here, and I am going to that place to find a wife and have a family."

The animals were silent. Man had long helped them with their small problems and they knew they would miss him – but they also knew they had no right to ask him to stay.

"We will find it strange without you, Man," said the lion, after the silence had lasted a long time. "When are you going?"

"Tomorrow," answered Man. "I will leave at first light. That is why I have called you together tonight, so that I could say goodbye."

"So soon," said the lion, shaking his head sadly. "But you must do what you think is best. Goodbye Man, I wish you health and happiness."

One by one, the animals solemnly said their farewells and left the cave, to return to their own homes. Soon Man was left standing alone and in his mind he went over all the animals who had just left. He thought there had been one of them missing but he could not think who it was.

"Why!" he said, at last. "iGola, the cat, was not here."

He could not understand this because the cat had always been closer than any of the other animals to him, sharing his cave and his food on many occasions. Going outside he called out to iGola. Many times he called but there was no reply and eventually he had to give up. The following day would be very busy and he would need as much sleep as he could get tonight.

In the morning Man tied all his belongings into a bundle. After a last look around the cave that had been his home for so many years, he set out along the path that would take him to the place where the other men dwelled. All the animals watched his going but they did not show themselves. Partings were sorrowful things. It was better that man should go his own way and forget his life as it had been.

*

iGola, The Cat

Man travelled for many days and nights before he came to the place where people lived in little, round houses with walls of mud and wattle, each with a conical roof thatched with long, dry grass. Everything was new to him and there was much to be learned but soon he had chosen a wife and had a house of his own, by which time the life he had lived with the animals seemed far, far away.

One day, when he had been out in the fields with his wife, tending the crops that were to keep them fed through the days of winter, he stopped to talk to another man while his wife went on alone to their hut.

She was inside for only a moment and then, with a loud, piercing scream she fled from the hut and ran back to where he was standing.

"Come quickly," she cried. "There is a fierce animal in our hut. Hurry and bring a big stick."

Man ran to his hut while the friend he had been talking to hastily snatched up a spear and followed him. Man could see nothing at first but then his friend cried, "Look! There it is in the corner."

Man looked to where the other was pointing and there, spitting and showing his teeth because he was frightened, was iGola!

"Wait," said Man to his friend, who had his spear raised. "It is all right, I know him. It is iGola."

He waited until the others had left the hut and then he went and crouched down before the cat. It was a very different iGola to the one he had last seen. His ribs were showing beneath his striped coat and many scratches covered his face and body.

25

"Why, iGola," Man said, kindly, "why are you looking so thin and scratched?"

iGola got to his feet and rubbed himself against Man's ankles affectionately.

"I was a long way from your cave when you left us, Man, and I was very upset that I had not wished you good luck in your new life. I have been seeking you since that time and have travelled far."

Man was very touched that iGola had taken so much trouble to find him. He called the woman into the hut. "Wife," he said, "this is iGola, the cat, who was my friend for a long, long time. He will not harm you. Please make some food for him, he is very hungry."

The woman was afraid at first but when iGola rubbed himself against her legs and began purring, a deep, happy sound that rumbled from his throat, she was not afraid any more and bent down to stroke him.

"How soft he is," she said. "There, iGola, you just wait here and I will find some food for you."

"Thank you for coming, iGola," said Man. "Now you are here I hope you will stay for a long time."

iGola did stay. Soon after his arrival Man's wife had a baby son, and as he grew older the cat loved to play games with him and keep him amused. He would roll over and over in the dust outside the hut, suddenly springing up to chase a leaf that was blowing through the village, and the child would gurgle with laughter.

One day, iGola spoke to Man. "Man," he said, "I came here to say goodbye but I like living with you so much that I would like to stay for always. Will you let me?"

"Of course," said Man, very pleased. "In fact, if you

were to leave now I know my wife and son would be
very unhappy."

And that is how iGola, the cat, came to live with Man.
But sometimes, especially at night, he will remember that
he was once a creature of the wild and will insist on going
out on his own, no matter how cold it is outside or how
warm it is by the fireside.

Where he goes only iGola knows, but he will always
return, rubbing himself against Man's legs and purring, happy that he came to find him many, many
years ago.

Two Wise Men

FATHER Kevin O'Kelly paused in his sermon to run a handkerchief between collar and neck. Soon the rains would arrive to dampen down this interminable heat. Until it did, even drawing breath was an exhaustting chore.

All around the little church he could hear the constant drone of insects. Inside, the scratching of a lizard scurrying up the rough, whitewashed wall sounded like the rapid ticking of a small clock.

Making a determined effort to put all minor, earthly irritations behind him, the priest beamed out at the pool of black faces staring up at him from the large congregation. Those belonging to the younger members of the tribe were as damp and shiny as his own.

Others were rough and corrugated, like the dried-up river bed. For these men and women the years of perspiration had long passed them by.

Replacing the handkerchief in his sleeve, Father O'Kelly resumed his sermon, booming out his words and sending the lizard scampering for the safety of the thatched roof.

"Yes, indeed. It says here, in the good book, that there was not a man in the kingdom. NOT ONE SINGLE

28

MAN, who possessed even half the wisdom of King Solomon . . ."

Seated close to the pulpit, Muvandi's eyelids parted. Observing that the Father's stern gaze was upon him, he nodded vigorously in agreement.

". . . So wise was Solomon," continued the priest, "people came from far and wide to seek his advice. People from beyond the city. Even beyond the bounds of the land over which he ruled. All who came to him with their problems – every single one of them – returned home well satisfied with the solution he gave to them."

Father O'Kelly waved a persistent fly from his nose. "On one memorable occasion – listen carefully to me now, for this will prove how very, very wise he was. On one occasion, two women came before him. They were holding a baby, a piccanin, between them. Each was fighting to gain full possession of the child, but neither succeeded. All the while, the baby, a boy child, was squealing fit to burst a tiny blood vessel.

"'Will you stop trying to murder that poor child and hand it to one of the guards,' said Solomon. 'Perhaps it will quieten and enable me to hear something of your problem.'

"A guard took the baby from the women. Immediately, they both began talking nineteen to the dozen, at the same time. They went on and on until King Solomon ordered them to be silent. Then he asked each of them to tell her own story. Not that there was anything to choose between them. You see, they both said exactly the same thing!"

There was a puzzled expression on Muvandi's face that pleased Father O'Kelly. If he had the old headman's attention, then the chances were that at least ninety per cent of his congregation was awake.

"Ah!" he said, "I can see by the expression on your faces that you are wondering how there could possibly be a problem if each of the women was saying the same as the other. Well now, I'll tell you. Each woman was saying that the baby belonged to her! 'It's mine,' said the first. 'This stealer of small children came along and took it from me.' 'Sure, and you wouldn't know the truth if it came up and put its hand down your throat,' said the second woman. 'The baby belongs to me, and to no other.'

"Well, for a couple of hours or so King Solomon listened to the women arguing back and forth, but neither of the women would change her story. However, wise King Solomon had the answer."

Father O'Kelly stabbed a finger at the congregation, "Do you know what he did? I'll tell you. King Solomon suddenly shouted, 'Enough! There has been far too much foolish talk already. Guard, hand me that great axe you're carrying.'

"'What are you going to do?' asked the women. Again, they spoke as one.

"'I'm going to do what I should have done two hours ago,' said the wily old king. 'Sure, I'm going to chop the baby in two. I'll give you each half, since that would appear to be the only solution.'

"Now, no sooner had the words left his mouth than one of the women fell down on her knees before him. 'Oh no, Great King!' she cried. 'Give my baby to the other woman, if you must, but please don't kill him.'

"Meanwhile, the other woman said nothing. Nothing at all.

"It was the first time the two women had disagreed and King Solomon smiled. He had found the answer he had been seeking.

"'Give the child to the woman who kneels before me,' he said to the guard. 'Then throw the other woman into the deepest dungeon in my kingdom and forget her. I knew the real mother would never allow her child to be killed. She would rather lose it than see it die'."

Father O'Kelly smiled, "Ah yes. The wisdom of King Solomon was great indeed."

No one in the congregation nodded more vigorously than did old Muvandi. Father O'Kelly had never before seen him so wide awake at this stage of a service. He felt a deep satisfaction.

Muvandi was always the last of the congregation to leave the little church. Closing the door behind him, Father O'Kelly fell into step beside the venerable headman and they made their slow way down the hill towards the village.

They had travelled less than half the distance when Muvandi felt in need of a rest. Choosing a large, flat slab of rock in the shade of a spreading indaba tree, he sat down. Father O'Kelly lowered himself onto the rock beside him.

"That was a good story you told today," said the headman, gazing at the peak of a distant mountain as he packed his old pipe with tobacco.

"You enjoyed it? I saw I had your attention, Muvandi. It pleases me greatly that you found it of interest. It's not every Sunday that you stay awake for the whole of a service."

Muvandi ignored the priest's criticism and put a match to the tobacco in his pipe. Talking past a cloud of sweet-smelling blue smoke, he said, "I, too, have had to make decisions like that one."

"I don't doubt it," replied Father O'Kelly. "The wisdom of a headman is gained for the benefit of his people. I hope the Good Lord was with you, just as he was with King Solomon?"

"Yes," said the other man. "There is one time in particular that I remember very well."

Father O'Kelly had known Muvandi for a long time. He was aware that a story was about to unfold. He settled down patiently to listen.

Muvandi shifted his gaze momentarily to the priest, to see that he had his attention. "It was many years ago. I was a younger man then and cattle were even more important to the head of a family than they are today."

He smiled reminiscently, "Aiee! Those were good days. I remember . . ."

"The story . . ." said Father O'Kelly, firmly.

"Ah yes! It happened in this very village, many years ago. I was called upon to decide the truth of two men's stories. One was a man who had married well. His cattle were many. They were looked after by his wives as though they were their children. The other man was a poor hunter. He would spend many weeks away from the village in search of meat – and it was scarce then. His wives were as thin and bony as whelped hyenas.

"One day, both men came to me, dragging between

32

them a fat, two-season-old bull calf. 'Muvandi,' said the rich man. 'This bull calf is mine but this lazy hunter, this slayer of old and dying buffaloes, has stolen it from me.'

"'He lies!' cried the poor man. 'It is mine and *he* is the robber.'

"They began to argue angrily between themselves and would probably have come to blows had I not brought them to order. I then asked whether they had come for the benefit of my wisdom, or so I might witness a blood-letting."

Muvandi smiled and smoke trickled from between his lips, "Men and women have changed little since the time of your King Solomon."

"True enough," agreed Father O'Kelly, "but surely it did not require a great deal of wisdom to decide to whom the young bull calf belonged? After all, one of the men was rich and well respected in the village. The other had nothing . . ."

"Things are not always as they seem," replied Muvandi. "As you well know. When one is father of his people then each man in the village is of equal importance."

Father Kevin O'Kelly raised a hand in acknowledgement of the admonition, "Of course. You are quite right, Muvandi. Please go on with your story."

"Well, like Solomon, I listened as each of them claimed to be the owner of the calf. Like Solomon, too, I knew that to the rich man, each of his cattle was as valuable as a wife. Each calf as a child to him. So I did the same as your King Solomon. I went inside my hut and brought out my old war spear.

"'Tie the animal to a stake,' I said. 'I will kill it and divide the meat between the two of you.'

"'Yes, that is fair,' said the poor man, eagerly. 'Kill it and we will share it.'

"The rich man looked at the bull calf. It had many years of growth left. Then he looked at my broad-bladed war spear, and he trembled.

"'No, Muvandi,' he said. 'Take your spear back to the hut. He can keep the calf'."

"Ah! And there you found the truth," said Father O'Kelly, triumphantly. "With such compassion for the poor creature there could be no doubting who was its rightful owner. You gave the calf to the rich man?"

"No," said Muvandi, knocking out his pipe against the rock and climbing stiffly to his feet. "I gave it to the poor man."

Father Kevin O'Kelly looked at the village headman in astonishment, "But why? It was perfectly obvious that the animal belonged to the rich man. Why give it to the other?"

"Because it was the right thing to do," said Muvandi, as they moved off along the path. "I have already told you, I am the father to *all* my people. The rich man had many calves. Many cows. The poor man's wives and children were hungry. Drought had driven the game far to the south. Had the poor man been forced to leave the village and go hunting to find food for his family, he would have been away for many weeks. During that time it was probable that his older wives would have died."

Muvandi smiled, a toothless smile, "You see, Father, there is more to making a wise decision than deciding

34

which man has the right of ownership. I have no
doubt that this King Solomon of whom you have
spoken, knew this also. You must tell us more about
him one day."

The Secretary Bird

THE meeting of the animals was in an uproar. Not one of them could remember the details of a most important item they had discussed only a few weeks before.

"This is a most unsatisfactory state of affairs," grumbled Lion. "We must appoint someone to take down all the details of each meeting. Now, whom shall we choose?"

"I suggest that you do it, Lion," simpered the jackal in his whining voice. "You are more clever than any of us and I am sure none of us could do it nearly as well."

"Quite true, quite true," agreed Lion. "But have you forgotten that I am the king of the beasts? Whoever heard of a king writing down details of a meeting?" He glared hard at Jackal. "That suggestion is quite ridiculous."

Jackal, trembling with fright at the look Lion had given him, slunk away and hid behind the trunk of a nearby tree.

"Well," said Lion, "we must have somebody. Elephant, you have a remarkable memory. Will you do the writing for us?"

Swinging his trunk from side to side and swaying from one leg to the other, Elephant thought it over.

He was rather pleased that he had been singled out in this manner but was determined not to let it show.

"All right," he said finally, "I'll give it a try, if you like."

"Good," said Lion. "Now, you run along and find some writing things and then we can carry on with the meeting."

Elephant did as he was told and when he returned the meeting started once again – but not for very long. Not only was Elephant very, very slow but he was also a terrible speller. He tried his best but after a number of interruptions when he asked how to spell such words as '*tree*', '*river*' and even '*lion*', the animals decided they would have to find someone else.

Elephant was rather upset and left in a huff, crashing his way through the undergrowth while the other animals looked at each other, wondering who should take his place.

"Why not let Monkey do it?" said the buffalo in his slow, deliberate voice. "He is very quick and rather clever. Let us appoint him."

The other animals agreed and so Monkey prepared to take notes of the meeting. Everything went well for a while, and as the others talked Monkey scribbled away industriously – but he was a rather irresponsible animal really and before very long he became bored.

First of all he began to scratch himself all over, and then began making patterns in the dusty earth with his toe. Suddenly, seeing that Tortoise was nodding off to sleep, he shinned up the nearest tree and threw little berries down onto the tortoise's hard shell, laughing noisily when the drowsy animal woke up with a start and looked around him to see who was banging on his shell.

Lion was furious and let out a roar that sent Monkey scuttling away over the tree-tops.

"This is quite ridiculous," roared the king of the beasts, as he watched the monkey disappear into the distance. "At this rate there will soon be no animals left here. There must be someone who is clerically minded."

"I know," said the bright squirrel. "Why not ask uDwayi, the bird. His spelling is excellent and he is a very serious-minded fellow. I am sure he would be most suitable."

Now, uDwayi was indeed most intelligent and he

could be seen at most hours of the day striding across the bushveld, working out such mathematical problems as 'How many ants make a hill?' or 'If three elephants met three hippopotamuses on a narrow path, how many moves would it take for one group to pass the other?' The animals agreed that he would be a wonderful choice and they set off to find him.

uDwayi was standing on the river bank with Ostrich, explaining with the aid of diagrams how the huge bird could build a nest similar to those built by the other birds for her outsize babies. He was rather relieved when the animals interrupted him, because Ostrich was insisting that she wanted to build it high in a tall tree and this posed problems that even uDwayi found difficult to resolve.

"Hrmmmph!" Lion began. He always felt nervous in the presence of someone who had great learning. "Hrmmmph!" he repeated. "uDwayi, we have decided to appoint someone to keep a record of our meetings and we all agree that you would be able to do it better than anyone else. Will you do it for us?"

uDwayi was not in the habit of making hasty decisions and he thought about it carefully.

"And if I accept," he said, finally, "will I have a vote on the council of animals?"

The animals were taken aback at this. The meetings had always been for the animals alone. To have a bird on the council with a say in their affairs was unheard of. Seeing their hesitation uDwayi went on. "You have had these meetings for many years without including the birds and yet you now come to me asking for my assistance. I won't even think of it unless we are invited and take our rightful place in the running of our land – well, what is it to be?"

Going into a huddle the animals hurriedly discussed the matter while uDwayi waited patiently. At last, after much nodding of heads they reached a decision.

"Yes, uDwayi," said Lion, "we have agreed. It will be as you say. You will be a member of the council and all the birds will be allowed to attend the meetings. Now will you accept?"

"Yes," said uDwayi, "I will, but as I am to occupy a position of such importance I must have a title. What will it be?"

"A title!" exclaimed Lion. "What sort of a title? We have never even thought about it."

"Well, it is about time you did," snapped uDwayi.

"Such a position is deserving of a title and I absolutely insist upon it."

While the animals looked at each other in dismay, uDwayi stood staring about him in a haughty silence.

"Really," said the slow buffalo, "what do you call a secretary?"

Lion jumped up, excitedly. "That's it!" he cried. "That is exactly what we want. uDwayi, you will be known as the Secretary Bird. Will you accept that?"

uDwayi thought the matter over carefully. Secretary Bird, Secretary Bird. It had a very nice sound to it. Yes, it had indeed.

"Yes," he said, "I accept."

And that is the name he has today. Striding on his long legs across the bushveld he always looks as though he is coming from a most important meeting and has a great deal on his mind.

Cheetah And The Rock Dassie

THE young world was a very pleasant place in which to live. All the animals were friends and, although they occasionally had disagreements, they would never think of fighting, or harming each other.

Indeed, there was only one thing to be feared – and that was fire. Not the safe, warm fire that Man kept in his cave and beside which the animals loved to lie, feeling its heat seeping into them during the cold winter nights – but the cruel, all-consuming fire that sometimes occurred when the bushveld was dry and brown; the fire that sprang up from nowhere, roaring and crackling across the land, destroying everything in its path. When this happened, all the creatures could do was run, never stopping until they had put a wide river between themselves and the flames.

One late afternoon, when most of the animals were dozing, the rhinoceros, who had a very keen sense of smell, raised his head, wondering what had awakened him. Scrambling to his feet he stood with his head in the air, sniffing first this way and then that.

He lumbered across to the sleeping giraffe and nudged him with his horned nose. "Giraffe," he said, "I smell smoke. You are taller than anyone else. Have a look around to see where it is coming from."

The giraffe spread his long legs wide and at the third attempt rose to his feet. He stretched to his full height and even stood on tip-toe but he could not see above the trees that were all about them.

"I am sorry, Rhino," he said, "I cannot see, but I am sure you are right, I can smell the smoke myself."

The rhinoceros snorted and trotted over to where the baboons were sleeping, all lying in a big heap together.

"Hey, wake up," he called. "Wake up."

The baboons, annoyed at having their rest disturbed, untangled themselves from each other and jumped up, chattering angrily.

"Quiet," shouted the rhinoceros, and when there was silence he said, "Giraffe and I can smell smoke. One of you shin up the tallest tree you can find and see if you can locate a fire."

At the word 'fire' panic broke out among the noisy creatures but one of the young males, with more presence of mind than the others, shinned up a nearby tree and with one hand to his forehead, shielding his eyes from the sun, he looked out over the landscape. He looked to the South, to the West, to the North – and he remained looking to the North, staring for all he was worth.

"It is a fire," he shrieked, "the biggest I have ever seen." Quickly, he slid down the tree. "We must tell all the other creatures."

Bounding and hopping across the ground he ran to where he had seen the elephant sleeping. Pulling the huge animal's trunk, a thing he would never have dared to do had it not been an emergency, he woke him up.

"Elephant," he cried as the big beast opened his eyes, "Elephant, there is a big fire coming from the North. The animals must be warned to run to the river as fast as they can go."

The elephant was wide awake immediately, and as he always slept standing up he had only to raise his trunk and let out a call that could be heard far away in all directions. Again and again he trumpeted, and as all the animals hurried to see what was happening the baboon told them of the fire.

In no time at all the whole area was full of animals crashing and leaping on their way to the river. The larger, faster animals carrying the smaller ones on their backs. Fortunately, the river was quite shallow and slow-running and was easy to cross. Secretary Bird stood on the far bank, ticking each animal off on his list as they crossed to safety.

By now, the thick, black smoke was rolling across the river in a dark, choking cloud and all the animals had been accounted for except the little rock dassie. Secretary Bird called the information back to the others.

"Oh dear," coughed the lion, his eyes smarting from the smoke, "where can the dassie be? If he does not hurry he will never escape. Look, the flames have reached the edge of the forest and will soon be at the river."

With a hop and a jump, the keen-eyed kite took off from the ground and was soon gliding over the oncoming fire. Suddenly, he swooped down and rose again, wheeling twice in the air before flying back to the others.

44

"I have seen the dassie," he cried. "He is sitting on the large rock by the forest's edge and seems too terrified to move. Even now the flames are licking at the foot of the rock. Someone will have to rescue him."

The animals looked at each other fearfully. They were all frightened of the fire and did not want to risk being caught in a bid to rescue the little rock animal.

"Hurry," screamed the kite, "or it will be too late."

Suddenly, there was a flash of tawny fur and the cheetah, whose coat was all one colour in those days, ran from the group of frightened animals and, without a word, plunged into the river, bounding through the water until he reached the other bank. Straight towards the fire he ran, sometimes disappearing from view in the swirling smoke, on and on until he reached the rock where the kite had seen the dassie.

The sparks, jumping ahead of the flames had already reached the area and small fires were burning everywhere. There, on top of the rock, with tears streaming from his eyes stood the poor, terrified, little animal.

"Quickly!" shouted the brave cheetah. "Jump onto my back. Hurry, there is no time to lose."

Peering through the smoke, Dassie saw Cheetah and with a mighty leap landed on his back and clung tightly to him. Through the sparks and the flames and the smoke ran Cheetah, running as he had never run before. Just before he reached the river the fire surged forward with a hollow roar and to the watching animals it appeared that he would be caught. But putting on a fantastic burst of speed Cheetah reached the river a split-second before the fire did.

Depositing the little dassie at the feet of the others, the cheetah stood before them, his sides heaving as a result of his noble effort.

"Well done, well done," the animals cried. "How fast you ran! No other animal could have run so fast. But look at your beautiful, tawny coat. The sparks have scorched it in hundreds of places. Oh dear, oh dear!"

It was quite true. There were so many scorch marks that his coat looked quite different. Cheetah was quite upset about it at first but in the days that followed, when he saw the animals pointing out the scorch-marks to each other he became proud to possess a coat with such distinctive markings.

The scorch marks are still there today and anyone

who has ever seen Cheetah run will agree that only he could have rescued Dassie on that fateful day.

What the other animals did not notice was that Dassie was also scorched by a large spark! Of course, they were far too busy praising the cheetah, but if ever you are fortunate enough to see the shy rock dassie, you will notice the black mark caused by the spark, right in the middle of his back, the black mark standing out from the brown fur.

A Matter Of Interest

.

ALL was in darkness around the small African village. From the river there came the impatient trumpeting of an elephant, a latecomer to the waterhole. Nearby there was the snuffling cough of a lion. His stomach full, he headed back to his favourite sleeping place.

In a little hut in the centre of the village a candle waged an unequal battle with the smoke from a charcoal fire. It succeeded only in calling attention to its own inadequacy.

Seated on the mud floor, close to the fire, was old Farikayi, the village headman. His thin legs were crossed, his lean, sinewy body hunched over a small pile of coins and a biscuit tin.

Farikayi's wizened face creased in concentration as the pile of coins grew steadily larger and the battered biscuit tin became lighter, rattling with a tinnier sound as more coins were tipped from it.

The old man was engaged in his favourite occupation: counting his life's savings.

It was not a large sum by European standards, only about twenty pounds, more or less. Even Farikayi could not have estimated it any closer than this, despite the many times he had counted it. When he was a child, education had been extremely difficult to come by. A few months' tuition at the Mission school had constituted the whole sum of his learning.

Things had changed a great deal since those days, Farikayi often thought. Now the children went to school for years, only to grow up dissatisfied with village life. They left as quickly as they were able and made their way to the towns. Here they worked all day to earn much money, only to waste it in the beer-halls every evening.

Ah! These young men! They thought they knew everything. Why, even the new missionary was a young man, full of silly ideas. Wasn't he always nagging at Farikayi to take his savings to the city and put his money in a thing called a bank?

Of course, Farikayi took no notice of him. A man should have his money in his own house. Be able to touch it and count it whenever he wished. Yes, indeed! He would continue to keep his money in the biscuit tin, buried safely beneath the ashes of the charcoal fire.

That is what he had told the missionary. The young man had replied that money put into a bank would grow and become more.

He must surely believe that Farikayi was a fool, to tell him such a story. Money was not a mealie plant that grew from the ground. It was not a cow that had calves. No, money was like the rocks that had stood, indestructible, on the top of the hill for many thousands of years. Neither growing, nor shrinking. This was the very thing that gave money its value.

Besides, Farikayi *enjoyed* counting his savings. As he did so he would remember how the coins had been earned.

The pleasant haggling that had frequently taken place. Sometimes whole days had been spent in small talk, with at the end of that time only a few pence changing hands. But they were good days for an old man to remember.

He knew that people discussed his money. As was usual with village gossip, the tales had become exaggerated. So much so that some talked of the hundreds of pounds he had hidden away. This pleased Farikayi very much. Such talk added to his prestige. It was of importance to a headman.

When the counting ritual was completed for another evening, Farikayi returned his money to the tin and buried it in its hiding-place. Carefully, he rebuilt the fire over it. Then, with a contented mind, he put out the candle and slept.

*   *   *

The next day Farikayi's presence was required in an official capacity, at the hut of one of his oldest friends. The friend possessed many wives and even more children. They were to discuss the marriage settlement to be paid for one of the daughters. She intended marrying a young man from a nearby village.

The day was spent happily, drinking and talking. Towards evening they were joined by the missionary who was to marry the young couple in the little Mission chapel.

When all the arrangements had been concluded satisfactorily, Farikayi took his leave. The missionary walked with him as far as his hut. He was witness to the scene of confusion that met Farikayi's eyes when he pushed back the blanket covering the entrance and entered his home.

Someone had been here in his absence. There could be no doubting the motive behind the visit. Farikayi's possessions were strewn everywhere and the floor dug up in a number of places – even beneath his bed. Freshly turned earth covered everything.

The only area left untouched was that beneath the ashes of the fire. Hastily, Farikayi dug through the ashes and into the earth beneath. He gave a deep sigh of relief as his fingers scraped on the lid of the tin box.

Who would have done such a thing? His mind recoiled from the thought that it could have been one of his own people. Then the answer came to him. Munjodzi! The young man had returned to the village only a few days ago. Rumour had it that he had been locked away in prison in the city for stealing things from the people for whom he worked.

Farikayi sent a boy to enquire for the young man. The boy returned with the information that Munjodzi had left the village hurriedly, no more than an hour before.

All this time the missionary had been watching, saying nothing. Now he spoke. Was this not the very thing he had told Farikayi would happen one day? Had he not foreseen this when he told him to take his money to the city and put it in a bank? The next time it happened, he said, the money would be found and Farikayi would be left with nothing.

The missionary said all this, and much more. Pressing home the advantage he held at this time. So persuasive was he that finally, and very reluctantly, Farikayi agreed to follow his advice.

51

When the missionary had gone, the old man sat lost in unhappy thought. But he had given his word. He would travel on the bus to the city and put his money in one of these things called a bank. He would go the very next day.

Farikayi took longer than usual over the counting that night. Tomorrow the money would be out of his hands. It would be safe, to be sure, but he would miss it. His evenings would seem long and empty . . .

*   *   *

The next day, Farikayi was up very early, walking to the road that was some distance from the village. Here he would catch the bus. As he walked with the biscuit tin clutched beneath his arm, Farikayi wondered what the city would be like. He had heard many stories about it, of course, but one could not believe all that was said by the men who had been there. They liked to impress people. Undoubtedly they had made up a great deal.

When he reached the road he had to wait for half an hour before the bus came along. The driver was a brusque young man dressed in a dirty uniform, but he was polite enough.

"Good morning, *Sekuru*," he said, giving Farikayi the deference his age demanded. "Where are you going? To the city?"

Farikayi returned the driver's greeting and said he was indeed going to the city.

He had taken some of the money from the tin to pay for the return fare. He took it from his pocket now and carefully counted out the correct amount asked. He was given a ticket in return, but he could not understand anything that was written on it. However, he had no doubt all was in order. The young man seemed to be quite efficient.

Farikayi slept for most of the journey, waking as they entered the city. And what a terrifying place it was! He thought he had entered another world!

All around him were huge buildings reaching up towards the sky, their many windows glinting in the sun. Wherever he looked there was movement and bustle. Motor cars were travelling in every direction and people were hurrying everywhere.

He left the bus in a state of bewildered amazement. Truly, the men returning to his village had not lied. Indeed, nothing they had said could possibly have described this place. It was beyond the comprehension of older people like himself.

As he stepped off the pavement, gazing up at the tall buildings, there was the screeching of hastily applied brakes. The noise that came from the motor car sounded like the trumpeting of an angry bull elephant. Farikayi hurriedly stepped back on the pavement.

He wandered around in a daze for a while, until the weight of the biscuit tin beneath his arm reminded him of the reason he was here.

A bank! How would he find such a place in all this chaos? What exactly was a bank, anyway? He knew only that it was a place where people put their money. The missionary had told him there were many of them – but what did they look like?

Farikayi wished he had asked the missionary a few more questions on the subject. The people here were in far too much of a hurry to tell him, even had he summoned up the necessary courage to ask.

It was then that a motor car drew up beside him. A man got out and put a coin in a strange-looking grey box that grew on an iron pole at the side of the road. As the man inserted the coin, the grey box made a peculiar whirring sound. A little black hand, like the hand on the missionary's clock, moved across behind a strip of glass.

For the first time Farikayi noticed that there were many of these grey boxes. They stretched all along the road. Even as he watched he saw three – no, four – people each walk up to them and place a coin in a little slot in the side of the box.

Sudden enlightenment came to Farikayi. Why, these must be the banks! Yes, of course. There were many of them, just as the missionary had said, and people were putting their money in them.

Having discovered the 'banks', Farikayi wasted no more time. The city was very large. It frightened him. He would leave his money here and return to his village. There, in familiar surroundings, a man felt like a man.

He took the lid off his biscuit tin. Extracting a coin, he put it in the slot in the side of one of the little grey boxes, just as he had seen the other people do.

It made him jump the first time. As soon as a portion of the coin went in, it was as though an unseen hand snatched it from him and pulled it inside. However, the whirr of the clock hand moving behind the glass amused him. He quickly inserted another.

Then a great idea came to him. Instead of putting all his money in one bank, why not put a little in each?

Then, if anything happened to one, he would still have lots of money left.

In no time at all he was happily working his way along the street, putting his money in the little boxes. He would put one coin in this one. Then one, two, or even three in the next.

Farikayi became aware that people were stopping to watch him and he puffed up with pride. Surely they had never seen a man putting such a lot of money in the banks before. He himself had noticed that other men put in only one or two coins. They must think him a very great man indeed.

It took a long time, but eventually Farikayi had completed his task. He still had a few of the larger coins remaining in his tin. He had been unable to insert these in the little boxes. Apparently the people who looked after the banks did not expect anyone to have such large sums to place in them at one time.

He transferred the remaining coins to his pocket and looked back at all the grey boxes in the street. Now they were all his banks. He had a brief moment of sadness, thinking of the empty evenings that lay ahead. The moment quickly passed and he turned away. The thing was done.

He could not see how the money could grow with no sun to shine on it, but the missionary had said it would. Farikayi knew the young priest would not lie to him. He felt a little more confident in the city now and with the empty biscuit tin clutched under his arm, he made his way to the bus depot.

The journey home was as uneventful as the ride to the city had been, but Farikayi could not sleep. He nursed the empty biscuit tin and thought of the money he had left behind, in the town. The next few nights would be spent in relating to the villagers all that he had seen in the city. But after that . . .?

All went exactly as he had foreseen. The villagers were suitably impressed by his description of city life. They registered satisfactory disapproval when he told them of the motor car that had made a noise like a bull elephant. But the subject was soon exhausted. His evenings grew longer.

He told the missionary he had taken his advice and banked his money and the missionary was pleased. However, it was all very well for the young white man to tell him he had done the right thing. The missionary had never really known what the money meant to Farikayi.

* * *

For two months Farikayi tried unsuccessfully to put thoughts of his absent savings from his mind. When sleep was long in coming he would think about it for hours. It was undoubtedly true the money would grow in the banks, but of what use was *more* money to him? He was an old man now. He had land, cattle and crops. There was sufficient to leave to his family when he died. Why was it necessary for the money to grow? It was enough to have it. Counting it had brought him much happiness.

The more he thought about it, the more convinced he became that he was right, and the missionary wrong. After all, he was not a child that he should allow a

young man to tell him what he ought to do with what
was his. Was he not the headman of his village?

There and then, Farikayi decided he would go again
to the city, much as the thought of that place frightened
him. He would bring his money back to where it belonged.
Back to this hut.

He would not tell the missionary, or anyone else.
Neither would he catch the morning bus. Instead, he
would take the one that passed along the road in the
late evening. That way he would arrive in the city very
late at night. If he caught the early bus home no one
need ever know he had been away from the village.

All went exactly as Farikayi had planned – at first.

He caught the bus and arrived in the city some time
after midnight. It was a very different city from the
last time. True, the tall buildings were still here, but
there were no angry motor cars coming at him from
every direction, and the streets were deserted. He much
preferred it this way.

It did not take him long to find the street where he
had left his money, but now he encountered his first
problem. It was not going to be as easy as he had
expected to reclaim his money. He could find no way
of opening the little grey boxes. They did not appear to
have any doors!

Failing with the first one, he moved to the next, and
the next. He tried banging them and twisting them. He
even attempted to uproot one so he could bang it against
the hard ground, but all to no avail.

He must have persevered for half an hour and was in the
process of prising one open with his old skinning-knife,
when a hand fell upon his shoulder.

It was a patrolling African policeman.

The policeman had been watching Farikayi with great interest for some minutes. It was no use Farikayi telling him to go away, that it was none of his business. Despite all his protests he was held in a firm grip and marched away, to a police station around the corner.

Here he was locked away in a cell and left until morning, when the policeman returned accompanied by a European who was called a 'detective'.

"Well, old man," said the detective, in Farikayi's own language. "You were caught last night by this constable. He says you were trying to force open a number of parking meters. What do you have to say about it?"

Farikayi drew himself up to his full height and looked up into the detective's eyes as he spoke.

"I know nothing of these things you call parking meters," he said. "I am not one of the bad men you have in the city. I am the headman of my village and a man of money. I came here only to take back the money I put in those banks, two months ago. I wish to take it back to my village, where it belongs. If it had not been for the missionary it would still be there and I would not be in this trouble. It seems these banks are very eager to snatch people's money, but do not like to give it back."

A puzzled frown appeared on the face of the detective. However, being a man who had grown accustomed to hearing things he did not understand, he sat down and asked Farkiayi to tell him the whole story.

Farikayi did so and the detective listened without saying a word.

When the story came to an end, the detective stared at Farikayi with a look of sympathetic disbelief on his face. Then he asked him the name of the young missionary. When he had it he left the cell, accompanied by the African constable, and the door was locked once more.

It was afternoon before the detective returned – and the missionary was with him.

They had a long discussion, the three of them. When it ended, Farikayi was told he was free to go. The missionary would take him home in his little car.

"But I do not want to go without my money," insisted a bewildered Farikayi. "I came here to the city to collect it. I have no wish to return empty-handed."

The missionary tried to explain the mistake Farikayi had made, but the old headman did not understand. He could not have lost all his money! How could it be? Was it not the missionary himself who had told him to put his money in a bank? Had he not carried out those instructions to the full? Surely they did not take all the people to the police station when they tried to get their money back? No, he did not understand this thing at all.

It was a very puzzled and distressed Farikayi who went to bed in his little hut that night.

* * *

On the fourth day after Farikayi's return to the village, the missionary came to visit him. He arrived with a spring in his step and a happy smile on his face.

"Farikayi," he said. "Farikayi, you have made me a happy man. The outcome of this little misfortune of yours has justified all my faith in human nature."

He held out a heavy canvas bag. "Here, take this. It's your money."

He went on talking happily about Farikayi's story being in the newspapers. Of money being sent by kind people to make up for his loss. Farikayi was not listening. He poured the money from the bag to the floor of his hut and could scarcely believe what he saw. Even without counting it he knew there was at least three times as much money as he had put in the banks in the city.

So the missionary had been right after all. Money *did* grow when placed in a bank!

He turned to the missionary who had finished his happy chattering and was standing beside him, beaming.

"This is my money?" he queried. "This is from the money I put in the banks?"

"Yes," replied the missionary. "It is your money – and I would not be at all surprised if there was not more on the way."

Farikayi shook his head in disbelief. Then a sudden thought came to him. How much more would this money grow if he took it all back to the city and replaced it in the banks?

He turned to ask the question of the missionary, but

stopped. No, the money belonged here, in this hut. Besides, what if it grew to three times three times? It was such a difficult business getting it back from the banks . . .!

Jan Van Wyck's Birthday

OLD Jan Van Wyck limped heavily from the house and stood leaning against a stone pillar at the front of the west-facing stoep.

Blue wisps of smoke drifted up from his blackened briar pipe as he gazed out across the valley. This was his favourite time of the day. The hour when the dying sun had almost completed brushing its evening colours on the foothills of the distant mountain.

It was a breathtaking view. One that Jan Van Wyck could see with his eyes closed. Yet today it brought him no pleasure.

The thought of what this day should have been weighed very heavily upon his mind.

Today was Jan Van Wyck's seventieth birthday. Many years before he had promised himself that on this day he would cease working the farm he had carved from the wilderness. It was the day he had always had in mind for handing over the house and the land to his two sons.

He sighed and wondered where his two sons were now. He had not seen them for eighteen months . . . No, it was closer to two years.

Two years was a very long time in the life of an old man.

Jan Van Wyck's Birthday

The Boer commandos did not pass this way very often these days. When they did, they brought only disappointment with them. The men he used to know, neighbours and friends, were long gone. Dead, many of them. Most who came to the farm these days were tired, bearded strangers. They were rarely able to give him any news of the two sons he missed so much. Piet and big Jannie were riding with a commando unit that operated far to the East.

All he knew with any certainty was that the war was going badly for the Boers. Even this news was many weeks old. Accurate, up-to-date information was hard to come by in such uncertain times.

The British had cleared farmers and their families from vast areas of the veldt. Deliberately allowing the land to go to waste, believing it would cut off a valuable source of supplies for the commandos.

Twice, British soldiers had come to Jan's farm in a bid to remove him. Instead of obeying their orders, he had barricaded himself in the house and threatened to kill anyone who tried to enter.

The soldiers had been new to South Africa. They had not put his threats to the test. They had ridden away again, but they had driven his cattle before them when they went.

This too, was a bitter blow to him. He had sacrificed many of life's comforts to build up the herd over a long lifetime.

He remained, an old man alone on a derelict farm. Fighting loneliness as he had so often fought drought and poverty. With courage and tenacity.

And now it was his seventieth birthday.

*

Jan had first seen this valley when he was a young prospector. He had camped on the very spot where his house now stood. He had watched the sun as he was watching it now and had made a promise to himself. The promise was that one day he would return and make the valley his home.

Fulfilment had taken him many years. During the intervening time he had met and married Marie, a girl from good Irish-Dutch stock. Together they trekked to the valley in an ox-wagon and here he built her a home.

She had been a good wife, never once complaining during those early, hard years. Living first in the wagon and later in the small wooden shack that preceded the permanent home.

Big Jannie had been born in that shack. Piet was more fortunate. By the time he came along, four years later, the house was completed.

Some good years had followed. A time when the farm was making a profit and Jan had two sons to share in the work and learn the lessons that were necessary to make men of boys.

Then came the bad years. First a virulent sickness swept through the African kraal, carrying off many of Jan's workers. Marie nursed them until she, too, fell ill and died after only two days.

Later, the rift that had long existed between Britain and the Boer Republic, widened. Eventually it became too wide to bridge. Animosity flared into a full-scale and bitter war.

Jan laid the blame for the war squarely on the shoulders of the politicians. The men who ruled both countries. Had they all spent more time farming there would never have been a war. What man would want to fight when he had a crop to be harvested, or a few hundred hectares of veldt waiting to be cleared?

All these memories and thoughts went through old Jan Van Wyck's mind as he leaned against the pillar on his stoep.

He sucked deeply on his pipe – and spat in disgust. He had been so wrapped in his thoughts he had allowed the pipe to go out. Taking it from his mouth, he fumbled in his pocket for tobacco pouch and matches.

The sun had slipped beneath the peaks of the mountains now, leaving a riot of colour behind it in the sky and deep shadows in the valleys.

Suddenly, Jan stopped his searching. He had detected a movement in the distance. Soon afterwards he heard iron-clad hooves clattering on the smooth, round stones by the dried-up spruit.

When the horses were half-way up the long slope that led to the house he could see the bright colours of the uniforms worn by their riders.

They were soldiers. *British* soldiers.

The old man spat for a second time over the stoep wall. If they expected a welcome in his house, or a soft bed for their officer to sleep in for the night, they were going to be out of luck.

He limped inside the house, shutting and barring the door behind him. Then he went around the house, checking all the windows. Pulling the stout shutters closed and securing them.

If the British wanted water, they were welcome to it. They would find it for themselves in the well at the eastern end of the farm buildings.

He had no wish to meet them. It was possible they were coming, as had the others, to order him to leave his farm. Well, they would receive a similar reception.

Jan took the long rifle down from its place above the fireplace. After checking it was loaded, he pulled up a chair close to the fire and sat with the gun lying across his knees.

He did not light the lamp. The flickering light from the low-burning fire was illumination enough for him. The less light the British saw, the better it would be.

Filling and re-lighting his pipe, Jan heard horses clatter into the yard at the side of the house. Then the jingling of harness as horses were allowed to lower their heads and crop at the short tufts of coarse grass, growing beside the fence.

Soon he could hear the murmur of voices. The sound was too indistinct for him to make out what was being said, but they were coming closer.

Hard-heeled riding boots clattered on the stone floor of the stoep. There was a brief pause and Jan discovered he was holding his breath. Then the room reverberated to the sound of a first hammering on the stout, wooden door.

"Hello, is anyone in there?"

It was a British voice. From the clipped, precise manner of talking, Jan judged it to be the officer. He took the pipe out of his mouth, but only in order that he might spit in the fire.

Jan Van Wyck's Birthday

The knocking was repeated. "Hello! Mr Van Wyck. Are you in there?"

Old Jan narrowed his eyes and frowned. One of the Africans in the kraal must have given the officer his name. He would find out which of them it was once the British soldiers had gone. Whoever it was would feel the sharp edge of his tongue.

The knocking on the door became more insistent. "Mr Van Wyck! Will you open the door, please? I wish to speak to you. It's about your sons."

The old man's mouth felt suddenly dry. Taking out the pipe, he laid it on the stone floor, beside his chair. Standing up, he discovered his legs were shaking alarmingly.

He made his way to the door. Once there he hesitated, unsure once more. "What is it you want to say to me? What do you know of my sons?"

"If you open up I will be able to tell you. It is extremely difficult to hold an intelligent conversation through a door."

Jan Van Wyck still hesitated. It might be a trick. A ruse to make him open the door. Once it was open they could rush in and overpower him. He did not delay for long. Anxiety for his boys overruled commonsense.

Removing the heavy bar from its seating, he flung the door open. "What have you come to tell me about my boys? What's happened to them, eh?"

The young officer standing before him was tall and slim and only lightly sun-tanned. He held his hat in his hands before him. This, and his short hair, made him look almost schoolboyish.

He had been smiling when the door was opened, but

the smile faded at the sight of the long rifle held in the old man's hands. It was pointing at his stomach.

"Quick, man! What about my boys?"

The young officer gently and carefully pushed the barrel of the rifle to one side.

"It's all right, Mr Van Wyck. There is nothing for you to be concerned about. Your sons are my prisoners. I captured them some miles from here but they implored me to allow them to come here to see you. They say that today is a very special birthday for you."

The old man stared stupidly at the British officer, unable to fully take in what he had said.

"What are you saying, man? Piet and Big Jannie . . . are here? With you . . .?"

The officer was given no time to reply. Two large, bearded men detached themselves from the group of soldiers standing outside the house and hurled themselves at the old man.

When he had regained most his breath after suffering their over-enthusiastic embraces, Jan Van Wyck blinked his eyes rapidly and cuffed his nose. Then he managed a shaky laugh.

"Agh! And did I bring up two great bears then? Come in the house and let me light a lamp, so I can see what men my sons have become."

As he turned to enter the house, he heard the young officer speaking to his sons. He spoke softly, but there was nothing wrong with Jan Van Wyck's hearing.

"I must remind you that you are on your honour not to attempt to escape while you are here."

The two young Van Wycks murmured that they would

keep their word and the officer walked away from the doorway.

Jan Van Wyck called him back. "Wait! Had it not been for you I would have been spending my birthday alone. That is not the way it should be for a man who has spent seventy years on God's earth. It would make me very happy if you would join us in my celebration. I have been saving some very special brandy for this day."

After a few moments' hesitation, the officer nodded his head, "It would be an honour to be a guest in your house, Mr Van Wyck."

"Good! Good!" The old man turned to his oldest son. "Down to the cellar, Big Jannie. Find some drinks for the soldiers, and the brandy I have been keeping all these years. Quick now, boy. We're throwing a party."

It proved to be a wonderful and totally unexpected evening for Jan Van Wyck. The British officer remained in the house for only an hour. Then he left the old man to talk of days past with his two sons. The lights in the windows burned until the sun showed itself behind the house.

As the British Army patrol was preparing to leave, taking his sons with it, Jan Van Wyck limped up to the officer and clasped him firmly by the hand.

"Thank you," he said, simply. "Thank you for giving me my sons for my birthday. I was able to keep a vow I made to their mother on the day she died. The farm is theirs now, but we made an agreement between the three of us. We are enemies now, you and I, but this war will not last for ever. When it is over we would like you to return. There is more than enough land for the Van Wycks in this valley.

We would like you to know there will always be a place here for you."

The warm rays of the sun were dispersing the morning mist as the soldiers rode on their way, the two young Van Wycks with them. They were prisoners, but at least Jan Van Wyck was happy in the knowledge that they would return when this war was over, as it soon would be.

He stood on the stoep watching them go, the blue smoke from his pipe rising slowly in the air of a new dawn.

The Swallow

THE black and white swallow flew high up in the clear, blue sky, wheeling and diving, his fast, pointed wings carrying him at a great speed. Swallow loved flying and never returned to his nest on the cliff-side until the warm sun was low in the West and the long, evening shadows were merging together. The other birds were envious of his splendid skill but the animals loved to watch him as he wrote his poetry in the air.

One morning, when the Summer was almost at an end and the late evenings and nights had become chilly, the animals missed seeing the swallow and they were very worried, wondering where he could be. The lizard said he would climb the cliff and see if Swallow was still in his nest. Up and up he went, his claw-like feet clinging to the rock.

Reaching the nest he poked his head inside – and there was Swallow. He did not look very well at all. The lizard called the news down to the animals, waiting below.

"Well, ask him what is wrong, Lizard," they shouted back to him. "Ask him why he is not in the sky, thrilling us with his flying."

"Swallow," said the lizard, gently, "the animals have sent me to find out what has happened. Why are

71

you not flying as you usually are at this time of day?"

"Oh Lizard," said the swallow, "I am so miserable. It was so cold during the night that I am not thawed out yet and I don't think I could even walk, far less fly. Please leave me now. Perhaps I will warm up later and feel like flying."

Lizard left the nest and returned to the animals, telling them what Swallow had said. They were most upset, it was so unlike the bird to feel this way.

"I wish there was something we could do to help," said the lizard. "He really does look terribly miserable."

At that moment the wind came along and, seeing the animals gathered at the foot of the cliff, he swirled up to them and asked them what was the matter.

"It is the swallow," they replied. "He is so cold that he is unable to fly."

"Well," said the wind, "I can do something about that."

So saying, he shot up into the air and headed straight for the sun. Up and up and up he went, passing so close that the sun's fiery breath heated the wind. Then the wind turned around and returned to the land, blowing into the nest of the poor, cold, little bird. In no time at all the swallow felt much better, and fluttering from his nest he stretched his wings and flew around for a couple of minutes before returning to settle on a tree above the animals.

"Thank you very much, animals," he said, "I feel lots better now, but I do not know what I will do tomorrow if the cold returns tonight."

"There is only one thing you can do," said the wind.

"It will remain cold here for many months. Tomorrow I journey far to the North, to a land where Summer is just starting. Come with me and remain there until it is warm enough here for you to return."

"That is a wonderful idea," said the swallow but seeing the sad faces of the animals he hastened to add, "Don't worry, I will return to you again as soon as I can and I promise never to forget you."

That night the wind blew warm around the nest of the swallow because it was a long, long way to the distant summer and he wanted the bird to have a good night's rest. The following morning, all the animals turned out to see the swallow depart with the wind, and they waved until he was nothing more than a tiny speck in the distance.

On his return, a few weeks later, the wind told the animals that Swallow had arrived in the far land safely, but very soon they had other things to think about because that Winter proved to be the coldest that anyone could remember and to the shivering creatures it seemed as though it would never come to an end.

Then, one morning, they awoke to the sound of a remembered twittering, high in the sky, and there was Swallow, swooping and diving over their heads.

"Hello, hello," he cried. "It is good to be back with you once more."

The animals were delighted to see him, but they were anxious too. "Swallow," they said, "why have you returned? It is so cold here, you will freeze."

"No," laughed the bird, "I came with the Summer. There will be no more cold nights for a long time."

73

And he was right, even as he spoke the animals could feel a new warmth in the air.

The swallow had much to tell them of the lands he had passed over, and especially of the country that had been his home for the last months. He told them of the green, green countryside and the animals so different from themselves, where nobody had ever seen elephants, or lions, or giraffes.

The animals never tired of listening to him and it was a delight to watch him as he darted about the sky above them. But one day he had gone again and the animals knew they must prepare for the Winter that was coming. They thought the swallow was very lucky to live where it was Summer the whole year round.

He still lives in the same way and the animals are always happy to see him because they know he brings the Summer with him, both here and in that other land, many, many flying weeks away.

The Fourth Wise Man

THE passing years had been kind to Mupatsi. True, he was no longer as agile as he had been in his youth, but time had laid a gentle hand on his mind. His wisdom was highly regarded far and wide and he gained great satisfaction from conducting the affairs of his village.

When he spoke to men on matters of importance, they listened to him with silent respect. As the headman, respect was his entitlement, but Mupatsi had known many village leaders to whom it was not given.

It had long been the custom, after the evening meal, for the men of the village to gather about a large, communal fire. Here, with full bellies and glowing pipes, they would speak contentedly of earlier days and exchange tribal gossip. Sometimes they might sit in silence, watching the blue smoke rise lazily in the air, to join the grey mist as it lowered over the peaks of the nearby mountains.

But in recent months the bellies of the men had not been full. They seldom laughed and now their talk was of only one thing. The lack of rain. There had been no rainfall at all during the last so-called 'rainy season', and it seemed this year might be the same.

Mupatsi had seen more than one drought, and none that had been ended by talk. Yet things were now becoming so serious it was difficult to even think about anything else.

At this time of year, with Christmas only a few weeks away, the rivers should have been full of swirling brown water. The fields green with juicy new shoots.

Instead, the waterless gullies resembled the forehead of an old woman.

The cattle, too, were suffering badly. If rain did not come soon they would die.

This would be calamitous for the villagers, and especially for Mupatsi. His very status in the tribe depended upon the number of cattle he owned. Without them he would be unable to buy wives for his sons and grandsons, or even pay the government taxes.

Yes, indeed he thought, a tribesman without cattle is a fisherman without a net.

Everything possible had been done to end the drought, of course. The villagers had paid tribute to their ancestral family spirits and to the tribal spirits, too. They had even organised a great ceremony to honour Mwari, the most powerful spirit of all. The ceremony had been conducted by the finest witch doctors in the land, and attended by no less than three headmen from neighbouring villages.

It would have been better had all the beer that was drunk been poured on the ground. That would at least have laid the dust.

At last, in sheer desperation, the villagers took to attending services at the mission station, much to the surprise and gratification of the young missionary, newly appointed to the district. Unlike his aged predecessor, the young priest had not yet begun to question the motives of his parishioners whenever they turned to religion.

No rain fell after the first service they attended. However, the missionary's God was not inclined to act in a hurry. The missionary himself told them so.

"For many of you," he beamed, looking down at the large congregation from the high box at the front of the church, "for many of you, this is the first service you have attended. It makes me very happy to welcome you. I can assure you that by turning to Christianity you will change your lives. Not immediately, of course. God does not work that way. But if you have patience, you will find He will surely answer your prayers."

Mupatsi translated this later to his fellow tribesmen as meaning that the villagers could not expect it to be raining as they made their way homewards.

Patiently, the villagers attended the services Sunday after Sunday. In long columns they would climb the hill to the little church, the music of the bell, swinging to and fro in its open tower, summoning them on.

But still the rains did not come.

During each service, due to the stiffness of Mupatsi's joints, he found it more convenient to remain in the kneeling position. Otherwise, it seemed he no sooner struggled laboriously to his feet, than everyone else sank to their knees again. He always remained one difficult move behind them.

It was this apparent display of devotion that led to Mupatsi's name being included on the list of those who were chosen to go to the city, on the mission's annual Christmas outing.

"You need not worry about it all being strange to you, Mupatsi," said the missionary. "I will be with you. It is going to be a great treat. We are attending

77

the evening service in the cathedral. Afterwards we will walk through the streets to admire the Christmas lights and decorations. I am given to understand they are the best they have had for many years."

Mupatsi was quite certain he would not enjoy the trip, but he did not want to refuse to go. It might upset the missionary. Then God would probably change his mind about sending the rain.

So it was that when the time came, Mupatsi boarded the coach with the others. He seated himself at the front and did his best to appear dignified. He stared stiffly to his front as the children, who comprised the bulk of the passengers, waved and shouted noisily to less fortunate friends and relatives.

It was a long way to the city. As the coach sped through the tribal lands Mupatsi could see the extent of the drought. Ribby cattle were everywhere, searching for paper-dry spears of grass among the dry, brown undergrowth. As it passed along its way, the coach sent up brown, powdery dust, billowing into the air in choking clouds.

Then, as the coach approached the city, the scene changed almost beyond belief.

The coach began to pass by houses where water sprinklers were flicking around, spraying showers of water over fine, green lawns. It seemed that everywhere he looked, there were flower beds riotous in their colours. There were even swimming pools in some of the gardens, in which children splashed and played happily.

Mupatsi was sitting bolt upright in his seat by now. This was indeed beyond all understanding. In the lands of his people, there was no water. Cattle were dying and villagers were in danger of starving because they could not grow crops. Yet here, in the city, there was water in abundance!

Mupatsi had no knowledge of the years of planning and building that had gone into the construction of dams close to the city. They ensured that its people and industries would never face a water shortage.

He only knew that here they had water. In his lands they had none.

Then the coach passed by a park. Here were large expanses of well-watered lawns, flower beds, and trees with luxuriant foliage. But there was something else. In the centre of the park was a fountain. It shot great plumes of water many feet in the air. When the water reached the highest point of its journey, it dropped back in the pond beneath it, having achieved – nothing!

All that evening, Mupatsi pondered on the reason for this apparent abundance of water, especially during the service in the great cathedral. Fortunately, the missionary was accustomed to seeing him on his knees for the duration of a whole service. It made it unnecessary for Mupatsi to watch the other worshippers in order to copy what they were doing.

He was able to think without being disturbed, and Mupatsi had been given much to think about. He felt there was something of great importance to be learned today. When the moment of enlightenment came, Mupatsi did not want to miss it.

After the service in the cathedral was over, the party began their sightseeing tour. Dusk was settling over the city and, as they walked slowly along the streets, the lights were switched on. First the normal street lights, then the decorations.

Even in his present preoccupied state, Mupatsi was impressed by the coloured lights. As the party turned a corner into the main thoroughfare, he stopped, suddenly overawed by the sheer beauty of them.

There were tens of thousands of bright, multi-coloured bulbs. Criss-crossing the street, they were woven into patterns of stars, crescents, Christmas trees, flowers – and a hundred other shapes. They transformed the city into a fairyland.

Delighted by the expression on the old man's face, the missionary said, "There! Isn't it worth coming all this way to see such a sight?"

Mupatsi could only nod his head. He did not wish to speak and allow his voice to betray the wonder he felt.

At length, the party arrived at the park where Mupatsi had seen the fountain. Here they inspected an exhibition of Nativity scenes.

Mupatsi had been following behind the others when suddenly he stopped and stared intently.

Before him was a life-size tableau, representing the arrival of the three wise men at the cattle shed where lay the Holy Child.

Presented by a large local store, the tableau was extremely effective. The baby was a doll from the toy department. The three, cotton-wool-bearded wise men were window dummies, suitably clad in silk dress material. In their hands, each dummy bore a gift, selected from the jewellery and cosmetic departments.

Mupatsi remained staring at the scene for so long that the missionary came back to see if something was wrong.

"What is this?" asked Mupatsi.

"This is the scene at the birth of God's son," explained the missionary. "The three wise men are overjoyed at his birth. They have arrived with gifts for him."

Mupatsi nodded, deeply satisfied. He had made an important discovery.

He made no protest when the missionary took his arm and led him after the others, heading towards the waiting coach.

All the way home, while others sang, or dozed quietly, Mupatsi's brain worked overtime. He was thinking and scheming, ignoring the happy songs of the children.

The following night, at the gathering about the fire, Mupatsi signalled to a number of the older men of the village. When each of them came to him, he whispered the same message. They were to come to his hut when the others had left the fire to go to their beds.

The meeting of the selected few lasted until the cold hours of the morning. As they left, some of the men could be seen shaking their heads doubtfully. Nevertheless, Mupatsi was well pleased. They had agreed to his plan.

*   *   *

On Christmas Eve, the missionary lay in bed thinking of other Christmases, and of other people.

He thought of his parents. They would be attending a midnight service in their local, stone-built church, in England. This had always been a highlight of the family's Christmas.

He had hoped to introduce such a service here but,

before leaving, his predecessor had suggested it might not be a very good idea, pointing out that this was Africa, not Bournemouth.

In England, the greatest hazard a midnight churchgoer might expect to encounter would be a drunken man, on his way home. In Africa there were lions, leopards and elephants, to name but a few species of the local fauna. Each, in one way or another, might possibly reduce the congregation.

As his thoughts wandered over Christmases past, and future, the missionary suddenly became aware of a noise outside. It seemed to come from the direction of his little church.

It sounded like the lowing of a cow and he frowned. He knew the villagers were very careful to shut all their animals in secure pens during the hours of darkness. Unless someone had been unusually careless, that was where they would all be.

Thinking he must have imagined the sound, he was about to resume his thoughts of home when he heard it once again. This time there was no room for doubt. It *was* a cow!

Throwing back the sheet, the missionary dressed hurriedly. Pushing his feet in to a pair of slippers, he quietly opened the door of his hut and went out into the moonlit night.

At first he could see nothing. Then he observed that the door of his church was open.

As he approached cautiously, he heard a noise from inside, as though something heavy had collided with the wooden end of one of the pews.

At the church doorway, the missionary hesitated. It

might not be wise to go inside if there was someone, or something, inside.

He listened for a few minutes more, but could hear nothing now.

There was only one thing he could do. Silently blessing the church authorities who had insisted the mission station be connected to the country's electricity system, he stepped inside the church. Groping along the wall, he located the panel of switches and pressed them all down at once.

The lights were not up to city standards, but they sufficed. In the yellow light cast by the naked bulbs, Mupatsi was tip-toeing towards him. Behind the old African, tied to a large carving of the crucifixion, was a full grown, if emaciated, cow.

"What on earth is going on?!" exploded the missionary, angrily. "Mupatsi, what do you mean by bringing a cow to my church?"

Mupatsi seemed embarrassed, but the missionary suspected it was only because he had been caught in whatever he thought he was doing.

"It is a present," he mumbled.

"Don't be ridiculous, Mupatsi. What do you mean, a present? You don't leave live cows in church as a gift to someone. Who is the present for?"

"It is a present for the son of God."

The missionary searched for the right words, "For the . . .?" He shook his head in bewilderment. "For the . . .? I'm sorry, Mupatsi. I feel this is something I *should* understand, but I'm afraid I don't. Suppose we both sit down and you tell me about it."

The two men sat on opposite sides of the aisle and

Mupatsi said, "It is a gift to the son of God, so he will answer our prayers and send the rains."

The missionary sank back in the pew, "Mupatsi, God does not do things for people because they give Him presents! He is not that sort of God."

"The present is for His son," Mupatsi doggedly insisted. "It will bring the rains. Did I not see it for myself when I went to the city? Here, in the lands of my people, nothing is growing because there is no water. In the city there is water everywhere! They have so much that they throw it into the air and waste it. Why should this be, I asked myself? Why should my people suffer when others have more water than they need?— "

"— Mupatsi," the missionary interrupted the headman. "The city has a great many dams built to maintain its water supply. It's . . . well . . . it's a very complicated process," he finished, lamely.

Mupatsi shook his head, "No, it is none of these things. When I saw the three wise men giving presents to the son of your God, I knew why. It is the custom of your people to give presents to a child when it is born. When I saw the three wise men – who are of your people – giving their presents, I knew why we have no water and your city does. It is because God is angry with my people for not giving a present to His son. I have spoken to the men of the village. It has been agreed that I should offer one of my cattle as a present. I know it is late, the son of God is no longer a child, but we have only just learned of this custom. God will understand."

The missionary was deeply moved. He sat in silence for a few minutes. He knew he must try to explain to the old man that his thinking was wrong, but he was at a loss how he should go about it . . .

"Mupatsi . . . What you saw in the city was just a tableau – a Nativity scene. The wise men were dummies. Make-believe wise men. It was there to illustrate a Bible story . . ."

Mupatsi stood up, his chin jutting forward stubbornly, "It has been discussed with the village elders. We have decided. I leave our present here."

This was Mupatsi's final word. Without a backward glance, he walked slowly out of the church and into the night.

The missionary watched him go. Then, with a sigh of resignation, he turned to the cow who was looking at him from large, uncomplaining eyes.

"Oh well," said the missionary to himself, as he untied the rope and led the cow towards the door. "There's nothing else I can do tonight. I'll tie this beast at the back of my hut for the night and decide in the morning what I should do. I have an idea this is going to be quite unlike any other Christmas I have known."

He was quite right.

When he awoke and went outside, there was no sign of the cow. Although he searched everywhere, it was nowhere to be found and he eventually gave up the search. He had probably not tied the animal up securely and it had wandered off, no doubt to be taken by some nocturnal predator.

The missionary carried out his Christmas day duties in the church, doing his best to shut out the events of the previous night. He had already decided that Christmas day was not the time to bring up the subject in church.

He would write a special sermon covering the subject, to be delivered the following Sunday.

The sermon was never preached.

On Christmas afternoon, the clouds built up steadily. By the evening, it had begun to rain. The sun was not seen again until the new year. By this time the rivers were filled from bank to bank with muddy, life-giving water. Fields that had been arid dustbowls, were now ankle deep in rich, oozing mud.

When the missionary went into church to preach his admonitory sermon, he found the small building packed from wall to wall with happy, smiling people. Folding the pages of his epistle, he dropped it to the floor of the pulpit. Instead, he preached a heartfelt sermon on the bountiful blessings of the Lord.

The young missionary had learned an important and salutory lesson: that God is inclined to make use of unorthodox methods to obtain results.

Mupatsi would, no doubt, have agreed with him had the matter been discussed. However, he was far too busy giving thanks to both God and His son.

He thanked the one for sending the much needed rain. The other for so generously returning his cow, which he had found standing patiently outside his cattle pen, early on Christmas morning.

You Can Take It With You

OLD Charlie was a bush-rat. It's a dying breed. Take any central African country you care to mention and you won't need more than two hands on which to count the number of old-time prospectors you're likely to find there now.

Most of them, like me, have taken the easy way out and succumbed to the 'Easy life'.

I nearly said, 'Given way to progress', but I don't really believe it *is* progress. Old Charlie certainly didn't.

"New fangled ideas," I once heard him snort. "There's no prospectors any more. Just a bunch of morons with noses glued to the ground and a metal detector clicking away in their ears. There's not one of 'em would recognise a gold reef if he broke a nose on it. Not without his machine, he wouldn't."

I don't think I replied. By then I had realised that Old Charlie was not the prospector I had once believed him to be.

Oh yes, he scratched a living, but it was not much of one. When you really get down to it, I suppose that was why I gave up that way of life. Left the bush – and Old Charlie – and returned to civilisation.

I had met Old Charlie many years before. Not long

after I found my way to Africa. I was a young man then, filled with a young man's ambitions. Looking to find my niche in life and hoping to get rich along the way.

It was in a bar a few miles north of Livingstone. It wasn't much of a place, really. A bit of mud and thatch, with a few sheets of corrugated tin thrown in. But the beer was good. Warm, but good.

I had worked my way north from Cape Town, doing odd jobs here and there until I found myself in this tiny, one-bar dorp. Leobula, I think it was called.

All the money I had in the world was in my pocket. It was probably just enough for a couple more warm beers.

Then, in walked Old Charlie. He came through the door hardly casting a shadow, he was that thin and scrawny. His clothes were ragged and stained with red-tinted dust. His face, what I could see of it through a thick, bushy beard, was the colour of the Zambezi in flood. The texture of his skin of a quality that only an elephant might have matched.

"Gimme a beer, Joe," he said to the barman, "And have one yourself."

The barman poured two beers, pushed one across to the old man and raised the other. "Cheers! What's the occasion, Charlie? Struck it rich this time?"

Old Charlie was too busy emptying beer down his throat to reply. Instead, he reached inside his shirt with his free hand and pulled out a small canvas bag, sliding it over the counter towards the barman.

When his glass was empty, he wiped a dusty arm across his mouth, expelled a deep breath, and said, "I reckon there's enough in there for a few more beers and some grub. Fill 'em up again, Joe."

He looked around the bar and noticed me for the first time. "Give the youngster one, too."

"Thanks very much," I said, "but I'm afraid I can't return the compliment."

He waved me into silence. "Don't suppose you can. Otherwise you wouldn't be sitting in here on your own, nursing a nearly empty glass. English, aren't you?"

I agreed I was English and before very long found myself telling him a lot more than I had told anyone for a very long time.

Old Charlie didn't say very much, except to call for more beers all round, now and then. We remained there, drinking, until was too dark to see. Then, when Joe made a move to light the paraffin lamp, he stood up.

"It's time I made a move. I've got things to do."

He looked down at me in the dim light. For a brief, uncertain moment, I knew I was looking at a lonely old man.

"You ever thought about prospecting, son?"

"Yes. Well . . . *thinking* of it's about all I've done," I said, uncertainly. "I don't know anything about it."

"Reckon you could learn, if you had a mind," he replied. "If you're interested, be here tomorrow morning and I'll take you with me. It's a hard life, but you're free. There's no one climbing on your back all the time, and you only have yourself to please. It's worth considering."

With that he stomped across the dirt floor and went out through the doorway.

That's how it all began.

The following morning, weighed down with supplies, I trudged behind the old man, away from Leobula. The

89

tall, dry, African grass closed in behind us and I entered a new world. Old Charlie's world. The 'Bush'.

No special considerations were given to you here because you were a human. You had to take your chances with the lowest form of life that wriggled through the rustling grass.

I've heard it referred to as survival of the fittest, but it's far more than that. It's a way of life that depends upon cunning, bushcraft – and common sense. Most times in life you're allowed one mistake, at least. There's none of that in the bush. Not that Old Charlie needed more than one chance. He never made mistakes. At least, not in the art of survival.

I wish I could have said the same for his prospecting.

It took a couple of years for the truth to finally dawn upon me. Old Charlie did not *want* to become rich. All he wanted was to live life as a nomad of the bush. Trekking through miles of uncharted bush country. Carefully avoiding the pockets of civilisation that were springing up all over the countryside.

Once I realised this, I became more and more dissatisfied. Finally, I voiced my thoughts to him.

He tried to brush my accusations aside, but I persisted. Eventually, he shrugged his shoulders, spat at a passing lizard, and said, "All right, boy. If it's bothering you that much, I reckon we'd better do something about it. If it's gold you want then I'll take you to where there's gold, but there's a lot more to life than money, you know."

I did not *want* to know. The next day we shouldered our packs and set off across country.

It proved to be particularly hard going. The rains had set in early that year. We spent much of each day slithering and sliding along tracks ankle-deep in mud, or crossing raging torrents that Old Charlie said should have been sluggish streams.

The nights were no more comfortable. We would crouch, shivering over a spluttering, half-hearted fire. Only the thought of the gold we would find kept me going.

After we had been travelling in this manner for ten days, Old Charlie halted, just short of the crest of a hill. It was about noon and the sun was high in the sky. He said, "Well, boy. You'll find your gold in the next valley. I hope it's what you really want."

I scrambled up the remainder of the slope, moving faster than I had for days. When I reached the top of the hill, my mouth dropped open in astonishment.

There, covering half of the valley floor was a huge factory. Smoke belched from half-a-dozen giant chimneys. Sprawled all around it were the houses and stores of a sizeable township.

"Well I'm damned!" said Old Charlie when he had puffed up beside me. "The fools have built their town over a fortune in gold. Who'd have thought it?"

I was absolutely furious. Right then and there I had my first and last big row with the old man.

To be honest, I was not entirely responsible for my actions. Somewhere along the way I had picked up a fever. Within the hour I went down with a severe bout of malaria.

I was told afterwards that Old Charlie carried me into town and dumped me on the steps of the factory hospital. I was never able to thank him. By the time I was fit again, Old Charlie was long gone.

I never saw him again. Not alive, that is. I found a job in the factory and stayed there for a while before moving into Livingstone and starting a little business of my own.

Some years afterwards, I received a telephone call from a Livingstone lawyer. He said he was acting on behalf of the recently deceased Charles Van der Kragh.

It was a couple of minutes before I realised he was talking about Old Charlie. My conscience bothered me like hell when I learned he had died, alone and friendless, in a native kraal, not ten miles from Livingstone.

I consoled myself with the thought that Old Charlie would have preferred to have it happen in such a way. He was a true loner.

The lawyer explained that, before he died, Old Charlie had made a will, leaving everything he had, to me. There was little enough of it. Nothing, in fact, but a small section of land, way out in the bush. A hill, quite worthless from a property point of view.

There was one condition attached to his legacy. The old man wanted to be buried on this piece of land. He had even left precise instructions as the the exact location of the grave.

It was the very least I could do for him. The next day I set off with two African helpers, to carry out his last wishes.

My newly acquired piece of land was in a wild and beautiful part of the country. Just the sort of place Old Charlie would have chosen to be his last resting place.

It was here I discovered for the first time that Old Charlie had possessed a remarkable sense of humour.

After the burial, I sent the two Africans away. Seated

on the ground beside Old Charlie's grave, I was not sure whether to laugh or cry.

As the sun set over the horizon, I opened my hand. The golden rays touched off an answering gleam from the chunk of mineral I held.

It was gold. Pure gold.

Old Charlie was lying in his grave surrounded by more gold than Tutankhamun ever saw.

He must have known about it, of course. He must always have known about it. Even in those far off days when we trudged, hot and uncomfortable through the bush, supposedly seeking the find that would make our fortunes.

I sighed. Then I stood up and placed the piece of gold ore in my pocket.

"Rest in peace, Old Charlie," I said. Then I turned, and walked away.

All right, so I'm a fool. But I remembered what Old Charlie was always telling me.

'There's more to life than money'. It was the way he would have wanted it to be.

Sungura And The Lion

THIS is a story from East Africa, a tale that is told to the children of a tall warrior-tribe as they sit half-dozing around the fires outside their huts in the dark, velvet warmth of evening. It tells of how Sungura, the rabbit, lost his long, bushy tail and was left with only the soft, white, powder-puff tail that he has today.

When the events related here occurred, there were no tribes in the land. In fact, the animals who dwelled there had never seen a human and they lived together happily – well, fairly happily. The trouble was that Lion had recently begun to realise how much stronger he was than the other animals and was taking advantage of it.

At first, it did not matter very much because he only proved his superiority over the others in small ways – such as insisting on drinking from the water-hole before them and having first choice of the shady trees in the hot afternoon sun.

But then one day he did something that was far more serious. It happened at that time of the year when many of the animals were having babies.

High in the trees that hung over the path baby monkeys screeched in mock terror and clung tightly to the short fur of their mothers as they leaped and swung through the branches, while on the path below a young wart-hog trotted along behind his mother, doing his very best to hold his tail stiff and upright as she did. Near the river, with father in the lead and mother bringing up the rear, seven ducklings in a straight line waddled, web-footed, to the water's edge. Lion saw all this and was very jealous. Why should these animals have babies while he had none?

One morning, when he was on his way to a flat, sun-warmed rock near the water-hole where he loved to rest, he was thinking very hard about the matter when suddenly a very faint sound came to his ears. 'Cheep-cheep, cheep-cheep'.

Lion stopped and the noise came again, 'Cheep-cheep, cheep-cheep'. Leaving the path and quietly creeping forward, he parted the long grass. There, crouching close to the ground, were three of the fattest, fluffiest, prettiest baby ostriches he had ever seen. When they saw Lion they 'Cheep-cheeped' quite happily, not frightened of him at all. Looking at them Lion was filled with admiration – then he had an idea!

Stretching himself to his full height he looked carefully about him. Good! There was nobody to be seen anywhere. Quickly he scooped up the ostrich chicks and hurried away with them.

Of course, you can imagine the fuss that Mother Ostrich made when she returned to the nest and found her children gone! Her cries brought all the animals running, and in no time at all they were out scouring the country for the missing chicks.

For two long hours they searched and were just on the point of giving up when who should come along the path but Lion – followed by the three chicks! Mother Ostrich rushed across to them but Lion picked them up and held them close, growling a warning for Mother Ostrich to keep away.

"But those are my chicks," she said, tearfully. "We have been searching for them for hours, ever since I returned from gathering food and discovered they had gone."

"Nonsense!" said Lion. "They are my children and no one else shall have them." And despite Mother Ostrich's pleas he remained adamant, refusing to part with them.

Now this was a very serious state of affairs and on such occasions it was the custom to call all the animals together to discuss the matter, and although Lion grumbled, he had to attend the meeting, bringing the three chicks with him. The Secretary Bird had been elected Chairman of the meeting and although he was fully aware of the importance of his position he was also extremely worried about being called upon to pass judgement on an issue which involved Lion.

Nervously he tapped his beak upon a tree stump and called the chattering animals to order.

"Hm, hm, hm," he coughed politely. "We have been asked to meet to discuss a matter of some, um, importance. In fact, no less a matter than to decide the parentage of the three chic . . . er, babies, that are with Lion. He says they are his but I understand that Mother Ostrich wishes to, er, dispute the matter, claiming that they are her chicks who so mysteriously disappeared this morning."

There was a loud snort from Lion. "Humph! Ridiculous! Of course they are mine. You saw them walking with me, did you not?"

He glared fiercely around the circle of animals who either nodded hastily or looked to the ground, avoiding his eyes.

"Well then," continued Lion, "there is nothing to discuss. If they are Mother Ostrich's babies then why did she not have them with her? That's what I should like to know. Babies follow their parents around, don't they? When you saw them they were walking with me, that should be enough for anybody. They are my babies and I defy anyone to prove otherwise."

Poor Mother Ostrich was most distressed. "But they are MY babies," she wailed, looking around at the others, hoping for some support – but to no avail. They were all too afraid of Lion to argue with him.

"It looks very much as though Lion has proved his case," said Secretary Bird. "But has anybody anything to say before we take a vote on it?"

There was silence for a few seconds and then a small voice piped up from somewhere behind the huge bulk of the buffalo. "Yes, I would like to raise one or two small points." And into the circle of animals hopped Sungura, the rabbit.

Squatting before the frowning Lion, Sungura settled his long, white, bushy tail comfortably around him. It was a beautiful tail, soft and silky to the touch.

"Mr Lion," began Sungura politely, "you have told us that these three babies are your own."

"Of course I have," roared Lion, angrily. "Everyone has heard me say so."

"Quite, quite," said Sungura in a soothing manner. "Then perhaps you will tell us how old they are?"

"We-e-e-ll," Lion was uncertain. "We-e-ell, you can see for yourself, er, they are just babies."

"Mother Ostrich?" said Sungura.

Mother Ostrich was not at all hesitant. "The oldest one, the boy, was hatched the day after the full moon and the two girls were hatched on the following day."

"Thank you, Mother Ostrich," said the rabbit, turning again to Lion as the animals murmured to each other.

"And which one of them is the boy, Lion?"

"What a silly question," Lion blustered. "Everyone can see that it is, er, it is – what does it matter? I am sure that he himself knows."

There was a peal of laughter from the assembled animals which ceased abruptly when Lion's tail started twitching slowly from one side to the other. Sungura rose to his feet now and began to hop backwards and forwards before Lion and the babies who were sleeping within the circle of his front legs.

Suddenly he stopped and began to shake his head sadly. "I don't know what the world is coming to, I really don't," he said.

Lion looked puzzled. "What nonsense are you talking about now?"

"Everything in the world seems to be changing," replied Sungura. "Take yourself, now. A noble animal. Strong, fierce, with a handsome head and a beautiful mane. More powerful than any other animal in the land. Truly, a king among beasts."

Lion puffed out his chest and looked around him to make sure that everyone had heard these words. Why, this Sungura was not such a bad fellow after all.

But Sungura had not finished.

"Yes," he went on, "you are all of these things, Lion. But if these babies are truly yours then how different the lion of the future will be. Instead of that handsome, huge head, they will have a tiny, comical one with a beak instead of a mouth. And that long, skinny neck – how can you have a mane around that? And the fur of the body! Why, it almost looks as though they will have feathers instead.

"Then look at their legs! Where have the strong, powerful legs gone? These babies do not have them. They do not even have four but only two each. Two long, slender things like young saplings!

"Why, Lion! I fear that these babies of yours will grow up looking just like – ostriches!"

There was a momentary hush and then all the animals

gave a roar of laughter such as has never been heard since that time. They laughed, and laughed, and laughed – all of them except Lion. His face became red, then purple and finally black with anger until, unable to control himself any longer, he jumped to his feet and forgetting all about the three babies, sprang at Sungura.

But the wily rabbit had been expecting just such a thing to happen and three quick bounds took him outside the circle of animals, and he began running for his life. Roaring ferociously, the lion chased him. Bounding up hills, sliding down into valleys, over streams, through the bushes and dodging in and out between the trees they went.

Before very long, Sungura found he was becoming out of breath and Lion's angry roars were getting closer. He decided he would have to resort to trickery if he was to escape. Ahead of him he saw a hollow tree that he was quite familiar with and summoning up a last burst of speed he disappeared into a hole in the side of it.

Lion skidded to a halt and, puffing heavily, tail swishing angrily, he inspected Sungura's hiding-place. Once, twice, three times he walked around the old, hollow tree. He saw the hole into which the rabbit had dived and, on the other side of the tree, he saw another hole.

"Aha!" said Lion. "He thinks I will reach into this one and then, while I am feeling about inside the tree for him, he will come out the other side and run away. But I will fool him. By reaching around the tree I can put my paws into both holes at the same time and catch him in the middle."

And that is what he did.

Lying down on the ground he put one paw into each of the holes and felt for Sungura. He stretched, and stretched but could not feel the rabbit. Then, with one final, straining effort he reached out as far as he possibly could and each of his paws gripped something that he felt sure was the furry animal – but he was wrong. What had happened was that his paws had met inside the tree and were gripping each other very, very tightly! He pulled and pulled but of course nothing happened!

Then, when he had almost exhausted himself, who should leap down from one of the branches but Sungura! Landing right by the tip of the lion's nose he said, "Ha ha! You may be the strongest animal in the land, Lion, but you are no match for Sungura when it comes to cleverness. Bye bye, Lion, I am off."

But this cheekiness nearly proved to be the rabbit's

undoing for, although Lion's paws were inside the tree, he had very large, sharp teeth and Sungura was only a short distance away. As the tormentor turned to hop away Lion opened his mouth wide and with a snap his teeth closed upon the rabbit's lovely, bushy tail.

Sungura leaped away in alarm – leaving the tail he had been so proud of in Lion's mouth. All he had left was a tiny, white stump.

Lion was highly delighted. "I will catch you easily now, Sungura, and it will be no use trying to hide among all your brothers. All I have to do is look for a rabbit with a short tail and it will be you."

Sungura was worried – but not for long. He was a clever animal and by the time he had reached his home he had thought of an idea.

His stumpy, little tail caused a great deal of interest among the members of his huge family, and brothers and sisters, cousins and aunts and even one great-great-great uncle came from far and wide to see it.

"But what has happened to your beautiful tail?" they said when they were all gathered together. "Where has it gone?"

Sungura shook his head sadly. "It had to go. As I was on my way home today I heard Lion talking to one of his friends. He said that he was coming here to kill all the rabbits and use their bushy tails to make a big broom to sweep the dust from his favourite flat rock. I thought that I would cut off my tail and then Lion would not kill me, and if I were you I would do the same."

There was great consternation among all the rabbits but they all agreed that Sungura was right, and with no more ado they all cut off their tails, leaving only a little, white fluffy piece. You can imagine how angry Lion was when he came searching for Sungura and discovered that all the rabbits now had short tails.

Even to this very day he sometimes remembers it and will roar until far into the night in anger. But he will never catch Sungura now because, as you all know, every rabbit has a tiny, white tail that twinkles behind him as he runs.

Of Faith And Father Shae

THE door of the little mud and dagga hut opened and Father Thomas Shae stepped out to face the harsh African sunshine.

He ran a finger around the inside of his stiff, white clerical collar and smoothed down the frayed edges of starched cotton that tickled his neck.

Shielding his eyes against the glare from the blazing sun, he looked out over the parched, yellow countryside. He saw, as he had on countless thousands of occasions, the undulating panorama. Broken by towers of ageless balancing rocks, it stretched for as far as a man could see to the purple-tinted skyline.

Here and there were dotted round, thatched native huts. They huddled together in pathetic little groups as though seeking refuge from the emptiness of the lonely veldt.

This was Father Shae's parish. The self-imposed isolation that had been his for almost fifty years.

It was to this spot he had come as a young man, eager to spread the word of the Lord to the tribesmen. He dreamed of converting them to Christianity. Of guiding their souls to a better world, even if their lot in this, the physical one, was lacking in the comforts of civilisation.

To this end he had dedicated his life. Many years before he had refused the chance to return to the green land of his birth. To take a sinecure, a parish where life would have been much easier. Where a parish priest was a traditional leader of the community.

Now he was an old man, bent with the weight of his lonely crusade among the still semi-heathen Africans in this particular area.

Oh yes, he knew many of them were Christians now – on the surface, at least! They came to church. They prayed. Under his patient tutorship they had learned to read the Bible. They even occasionally brought their children, small brown squalling bundles of nakedness, to him for christening.

But once back in their small villages, tradition was all-powerful. When a villager died, he was not buried in the small square of consecrated ground behind the church. He would be taken out to the veldt, where the ceremonies of countless years of paganism were re-enacted to send the deceased on his way. To join his father, grandfathers and great-grandfathers who had been dispatched in a similar fashion to join their ancestors.

Yet Father Shae had tried, and was still trying, to make them believe as he himself believed. To tread the path that would lead to ultimate salvation.

He turned away from the sun and walked along the well-worn path to the church. *His* church!

His heart swelled within him as he approached this monument to his devotion. Here was something he *had* achieved. The compact, grey stone building was his own creation. The result of many years of hard labour. Every stone shaped and cemented in place by his own hands.

The church was something that was admired by all who came this way. Even the bishop of the scattered diocese had been impressed by this evidence of one man's faith and tenacity.

"Father Shae," he had said, "when many other, more exalted servants of the Lord have been forgotten, your name will live on in this church. It is something of which you may be very proud. A permanent oasis of faith in this land thirsting for the words of salvation."

Even the wooden pews, planed to a fine smoothness, were his own work. Walking down the narrow aisle towards the altar, Father Shae let his hand rest gently upon their unvarnished finish.

Today was Sunday. In a few hours time these seats would be filled with his flock. Their chattering, fidgeting children unsubdued by the admonishments of their parents.

Father Shae smiled at the thought of them. To him they were all children. Even their aged chief was some years his junior.

He made his way to the tiny vestry. This was where he would write his sermon. It would be a simple one, in words they could understand. He would bring to it something from their everyday life. Perhaps one of their daily tasks. Whenever they carried it out they might remember his words and their creator and move a fraction closer to Christianity.

The vestry was a cool room, its thick stone walls keeping out much of the heat of the day. Here Father

Shae always remained until it was time for the service to begin. Here he would write, re-write, think and pray.

Going to a cupboard, he brought out paper, ink, and the pen with a scratchy nib, with which he always wrote his sermons. Indeed, it was now the only pen he possessed.

Setting them out in front of him, he pulled up a stool. Before settling down to write, he rested his elbows on the table and clasped his hands together. Leaning his head upon them, he prayed, silently and sincerely.

He sat deep in thought for a long time before he made up his mind. Today his sermon would be about love. The love of God for his people. The love that men should have towards one another. Perhaps in this way he might impart some of the love he had for these people and, yes, towards this harsh, primitive country too.

He wrote, head bowed, the pen scratching its way across the paper. Large, sprawling handwriting filling the pages as he toiled through the afternoon.

He had almost finished now. His eyes scanned the last paragraph he had written.

'So you see, love is all embracing. All powerful. Love begets love. If you love your fellow man, then he in turn will eventually learn to love you. Then will come the peace and understanding that is good in the eyes of the Lord.'

Suddenly, Father Shae heard the sound of smashing wood. It came from inside the church, beyond the vestry door.

He had thought he heard voices some minutes earlier

but glancing at his watch, the only luxury he allowed himself, he knew it was far too early for anyone to be arriving for the service. He believed he must have imagined the sound.

Now he realised he had not been mistaken. There *was* someone in his church – and they had not come for the service.

The noise he had heard before was repeated. This time the splintering of wood was followed by another sound as something crashed heavily to the floor.

Father Shae rose to his feet, bewilderment on his lined old face.

Hurrying to the vestry door, he threw it open. He was brought up short in the doorway, unable to fully take in the scene that met his eyes.

There were six Africans in the church, all strangers to him. Using axes, they were systematically smashing the pews he had so lovingly created. His pulpit lay on its side as one of the intruders chopped at it frantically.

They had not seen him and he started towards them, the pages of the sermon in his hand. He stumbled on a piece of broken woodwork and, startled by his unexpected appearance, the men stopped their work of destruction.

"What on earth do you think you're doing? Who are you? What right do you think you have to come in here and smash up my church like this?" The priest's voice rang out in the desecrated place of worship.

One of the Africans, a huge man with a pock-marked face and bloodshot eyes took a pace forward.

"You, a white man, ask us what right we have to be here? This is our country. It is you who should ask yourself that question. What right have *you* to be here?"

Father Shae stopped, halted as much by the look of sheer hatred on the man's face as by his menacing attitude.

So that was what this was about! Even in this isolated spot he had heard rumours of unrest in other parts of the country. It had been brought about by small groups of men who sought power by kindling the destructive fires of tribalism and racialism. He had heard about it, but had quickly dismissed it from his mind.

The troubles were political, and politics had no place in his life. Now he had come face to face with it, here in his own little church.

Father Shae was too old to deal with such a situation. Poverty he could fight. Hardship, too. But lawless, hate-filled men were outside his sphere of experience. He would never understand them.

He stared at the big man for what seemed an eternity, not speaking. Then, shaking his head, he looked down at the splintered furnishings strewn about the floor of his church.

Turning back to the wild-eyed man, he pointed to the door. "Go, my children," he said, brokenly. "Go away in peace. The Lord will forgive you, I can only try."

Wearily, he moved away from the vandals. Pushing aside the splintered wreckage with his feet, he made his way to the altar.

Dropping heavily to his knees, he began to pray, ignoring the men who stood at the back of the church.

Stirred by memories of earlier days spent in mission schools, the Africans stood in silence for a while. Then, quietly and sheepishly, they turned and filed from the church.

Only the big man remained, glowering at the back of this little old man. By his very humility and acceptance of defeat, he had won a victory. Then the big man walked slowly and uncertainly towards the door.

As he reached it, he stopped and turned. A wild look of uncontrollable rage crossed his face. Drawing back his arm, he hurled his axe at the old man kneeling before the altar.

The force of the blow knocked Father Shae forward, face down on the floor. He tried to rise, but succeeded only in rolling half over on to his side. The axe, protruding from his back, prevented him from rolling further.

Reaching out, he groped for something . . . anything . . . with which to pull himself up. His outstretched fingers grasped the altar cloth. As he tugged it towards him, something crashed heavily to the floor.

Slowly and painfully turning his head, he saw the crucifix lying near to him, just within reach of his rapidly weakening hand. His fingers closed about it and he drew it up to his breast.

With the familiar symbol of his faith clutched close, he felt strangely at peace. He began to pray.

His thoughts strayed to that other Thomas, who had died while he was praying in front of his altar in Canterbury. Slain by men who did not understand. Men who believed that what they were doing was right.

It was too much to hope that his death would have as far-reaching an effect as had the death of Becket. Yet it might help, if only in a very small way.

*

When the villagers fearfully entered the church, they found Father Shae lying with the cross clasped tightly in lifeless hands. The papers of his sermon were strewn all about him, stained with his own blood. The words of love obliterated by the deed of hate.

Stunned by the senseless murder, the villagers gathered about him, not knowing what they should do.

It was their headman who made the decision for them.

He did what Father Shae would have wished him to do. That which had been done in this place for fifty years. Which he, the headman, would see was carried on by his tribe for all time.

He fell to his knees. Calling on the others to do the same, he began, "*Our Father, which art in Heaven, hallowed be thy name . . .*"

The prayer swelled in volume as more and more of his people joined in.

It was the sound of the seed sown by Father Shae, bursting forth. Pushing its way upward through what had once been stony ground . . .

God's Good Day

"THE day is fine, Father."

From behind the struggling hedge that surrounded the Mission's meagre flower garden, the grey-haired priest straightened to a standing position. As he did so, his left hand sought the small of his back, the fingers of his other hand easing their grip on the secateurs.

He frowned as he looked into the wizened face over the hedge. A face that was split in a toothless smile.

"The day is as God gives it to us, Chivoko. It's men who make it good, or bad."

The old man nodded vigorously at these words of wisdom, "Yes, Father. The day is good."

Father McCabe sighed. Reaching out, he placed the pruning-shears on the stump of a blue gum tree. He had felled the tree with a hand axe, almost forty years before.

"And what is it good for today, Chivoko?" he asked, rubbing the stiff fingers of his right hand as he spoke. "Would it be for drinking, perhaps? Or for gambling outside the trading store?"

Chivoko's face assumed a pained expression. Although the hedge was between them, the priest knew that the other man would be shuffling his feet nervously.

"No, Father. None of these things. Today would be a good day for going to see the sister of my mother, who has many years and is very, very sick."

"Then go with my blessing," said the priest, reaching out towards the tree stump. "I would not want to delay one who sets out with such noble intentions."

"But, Father," Chivoko said hurriedly. "The way is long. All the way to the city. I shall need to travel on the bus from the village."

"Then there is even more need for haste," declared Father McCabe, unsympathetically. "Unless they've changed the time of the bus, I believe it's due to leave in an hour."

Chivoko's face registered dismay. "It leaves in an hour, as you say, but unless I can find money for the bus fare I will not be able to go with it. The sister of my mother, who is sick, will be alone, with no one to visit her."

Father McCabe glared angrily at the old man, "It's just as I thought! You are after money, Chivoko. Well, you'll have no more from me. What happened to the last five shillings I gave to you?"

Chivoko hung his head and said nothing.

"In case you've forgotten, I'll remind you. You wanted money to buy food for the children of one of your numerous relatives. It all went on drink, I believe?"

The old man avoided the priest's eyes, "It was a long walk in the hot sun to the store, Father. It made me very thirsty."

"And the time before that?" the priest continued, "You needed seeds, in order to grow food for your family. What happened to that money? I seem to recall it went on gambling."

113

"It is true, Father. That is how the money was spent. But this time it is different. The sister of my mother is very ill indeed. I wish to see her and buy her something. She is very old."

"Of course," said Father McCabe. "She would be. But how did you receive the news she was ill? Do you have a letter I can see?"

The old man's face screwed up in a perplexed frown for a few seconds, "Ah, no, Father. It was told to me by a son of my brother. He passed through here only yesterday. It was he who told me of this. He said she wishes to see me. I must go, Father."

Father McCabe looked at the old man for a few moments. Then he shook his head in an admission of defeat.

"All right, Chivoko. How much do you need?"

The old man flashed his toothless smile once more. "Thank you, Father. Fifteen shillings should be enough, I think."

"Fifteen shillings? The bus fare is only five!"

"Yes, of course," Chivoke spoke hastily, realising his error, "but I wish to buy things for her. "Twelve and sixpence, perhaps?"

"I'll give you ten shillings," said the priest. "Come around to the front of the Mission and I'll fetch it."

Standing outside the door, the old man held out both hands to receive the money that the priest placed in them.

"There you are, Chivoko. If I find out you've misspent it you'll never have another penny from me. This money doesn't come easily."

"Thank you, Father." The old man bobbed his thanks as he backed away. "It shall be spent well."

"Be sure of that," the priest raised his voice to reach the departing figure. "That's God's money I've given you. He'll be watching to see what you do with it."

Father McCabe shook his head as he watched the old man hurry away at a speed that belied his age. He knew he was foolish to give money to Chivoko. The old man had never put a penny to any good purpose.

Many years before, Chivoko had been a fine hunter. Then, during the war years, he had been an army tracker in the jungles of the Far East. On his return, when others were buying cattle and lands with their gratuities, Chivoko had gone on a wild drinking spree that lasted for months. He did not return to his village until all the money was gone.

As far as Father McCabe knew, Chivoko had never done an honest day's work since that time.

The battered old car rattled past the Mission garden and Chivoko crouched low, trying to lose himself amidst the laughing, protesting passengers.

The owner of the vehicle, a retired police sergeant, charged only a shilling per person for the journey to the city. Not unnaturally, this was the villagers' first choice of transport. None of them took the bus unless the sergeant's car was full to bursting point.

On the way to the city the ancient vehicle groaned its way to the top of even the most modest incline and careered down the other side. It bounced through potholes and swayed alarmingly around bends before it finally left the dirt roads behind and joined a steady flow of vehicles heading towards the race-course.

Once in the car park it was distinguishable from the hundreds of other vehicles by the wisps of steam hissing through holes in the radiator.

Paying his small entrance fee at the turnstile, Chivoko pushed his way through the crowds to study the board alongside the tote.

When he was satisfied, he filled in a form and handed it in at the window marked 'Jackpot Entries'. Then, after placing a small bet on the first race, he pushed his way through the noisy crowds until he found a position close to the rails.

Chivoko loved horse-racing. He enjoyed the jostling crowds, the suppressed excitement that exploded into noise when the gates of the starting boxes flew open. Most of all, he enjoyed seeing the horses pounding over the turf with their colourfully-clad riders urging them on.

Today was a grand day's racing. The sun was warm, the crowd happy, and the beer was good.

If Chivoko's conscience bothered him at the thought of the source of his money, he did not allow it to spoil his enjoyment.

*   *   *

On Monday afternoon, Father McCabe was drawing water from the well in his garden, when Chivoko opened the wicket-gate and made his way towards him.

The priest's lips drew together in a thin line of disapproval and he wound the bucket up from the depths of the well, as though he had not seen his visitor.

Even when the old African shuffled to a halt not two paces away and coughed politely, the priest refused to acknowledge his presence.

Three times the bucket dropped down the well and three times it was wound up, the contents emptied into a large wooden tub standing at the edge of the well. Only then did the priest speak to the old man.

"If you are after more money, Chivoko, the answer is an emphatic NO!"

"I have not come for money, Father."

The priest's eyebrows shot upwards in an expression of exaggerated surprise, "Not for money? Then perhaps it is to ask me to pray for the sick sister of your mother? How is she? I saw you going past in Mangwende's motor car on Saturday. I understand he was on his way to the races? I trust you found a few minutes to visit her when the races ended?"

Chivoko fidgeted, ill-at-ease, "Yes, Father. I went to see her. Happily, she was not as sick as I had been told."

"Really? Perhaps it is just as well. Doubtless all your money had gone by the time you arrived at her house."

Chivoko looked directly at the priest, "No. I took some things for her. It is the way of my people to take care of the family. To give to those who have less than themselves."

"Oh!" Father McCabe was temporarily lost for words. "I am sorry, Chivoko. I've misjudged you. When I saw you going past in the motor car, trying to hide yourself from me, I thought the money I had given to you would be spent at the races."

"You did not misjudge me, Father. I *did* go to the races." Reaching in a pocket, the old man drew out an envelope and thrust it towards the priest. "Here, Father. This is for you."

Puzzled, the priest opened the envelope. When he saw the contents, he gasped and almost dropped it in his surprise. It was full of crisp, new, five pound notes.

"Wh . . . what's this? There must be at least a hundred pounds here!"

"Two hundred," Chivoko corrected him. "You see, Father, at the races I won what they call the 'jackpot'. It was much money. More than I ever dreamed of winning. It was fortunate that Mangwende was with me. He was once a policeman, as you know, and he understands about such things. He made me stay in the city until this morning. Then he took me to see a man who is a bank manager. This man is keeping my money for me. When I need some more I have only to go and ask him for it. I let him keep the money, but told him I wanted two hundred pounds for you. You called to me on Saturday, as I left you, and said it was God's money you had given to me. As I was lucky and won so much money, it is only right that God should be lucky too. So I have brought this money for you to give to him."

The priest could only stare at Chivoko. His mouth moved as though he was speaking, but no sound came forth.

At the gate, Chivoko turned and smiled his toothless smile.

"As you told me, Father, the day is as God gives it to us. It was a good day."

uTshwebe And The Monkey

THE sounds of frantic squawking and excited chattering came from the large umbrella tree alongside the river and, complaining bitterly and shedding feathers as she went, uTshwebe, the Jacana bird, flew from the tree to the far side of the river.

The monkey, clutching a handful of tail-feathers, watched her go, gleefully dancing up and down on a large branch. This was his favourite game. He would hide in the long grass, carefully noting where the little bird settled and, creeping up on her very, very quietly, would suddenly leap out and grab some more of uTshwebe's feathers.

Not unnaturally, the bird was quite upset about it but she could think of no way to put an end to the monkey's tricks. It did not matter where she settled, in a tree, on the ground or on a rock, he always found her.

One day, when she was strolling alongside the river, nervously looking over her shoulder, who should she meet but the Great God, coming in the opposite direction.

"Good morning, uTshwebe," the Great One said. "Why! Whatever is the matter with you? Where have all your tail feathers gone? What can have happened to make you look so bedraggled?"

The Jacana looked very sad. "It is the monkey," she said. "He is always hiding and, when I am least expecting it, he leaps out and plucks some of my feathers."

"Hmmmm!" said the Great God, a frown appearing on his usually happy face. "This will not do at all. Now, let me see, what can be done about it?"

He stood stroking his chin as he thought about the problem.

"I suppose I could move you to the mountains," he said, more to himself than to the bird. "But – no, that would not do, since you gather your food from the lake. I could make you so large that the monkey would be afraid of stealing your feathers – but that would be a great pity, for you are most attractive as you are. No, it will have to be something else, something that will teach the monkey a lesson he will not forget."

Suddenly he snapped his fingers. "I think I have the answer. Come closer, uTshwebe."

The bird approached very close and the Great God whispered into her ear. After a few moments uTshwebe drew back, looking rather doubtful, but the Great God beckoned her forward again. He whispered some more and very soon the bird started to laugh.

"Yes," she said, "that will be the perfect answer. Then I will be able to stay here, where I am happy, and the monkey will be punished. Yes, I agree."

And so it was, that very same night, when all the animals and birds were sleeping, uTshwebe went off to meet the Great God, as they had planned.

What happened, nobody but themselves ever knew, and they never told.

The next morning, when the monkey woke up he thought he would look for the bird and have some more fun. He looked across the bushveld, but she was not there. He crept up into the bird's favourite tree but she was not there either. He was rather puzzled and then, when he was walking along the path near the lake, he saw her walking along with her head down, on the far side of a large clump of grass.

He grinned to himself and crept quietly towards her, hidden from view by the long grass. He took a quick look. Yes, she was still there, he could just see the top of her back. Tensing himself he suddenly sprang at her, letting out a screech of delight – but the screech turned into a gurgle as, to his great dismay, he landed with a splash and disappeared beneath the surface of the lake!

With many cries of alarm, he floundered to the bank and pulled himself ashore. He stayed there for a long time, spitting out the water he had swallowed and recovering from his fright.

When he felt better he looked to see where the bird was – and received a shock. There was uTshwebe walking on the water!

He was most astonished. "uTshwebe!" he cried. "How is it you are able to walk upon the water, like that?"

"Oh," said uTshwebe, casually, "it is quite simple. You made the mistake of jumping in, Monkey. The way to do it is to put one foot on the water and walk quickly, then you too will be walking on the water, as I am."

The monkey was doubtful at first but then he looked again at the bird and thought, It must be true. That is what uTshwebe is doing.

He stepped out onto the surface of the lake – and with a gurgle disappeared beneath the water once again! This time, when he had struggled to the bank and lay gasping and coughing out water and weed, he was very angry to hear uTshwebe laughing at him.

"That serves you right, Monkey," said the bird. "That is payment for the many times you have pulled my feathers out. Do not bother to try walking on the water again, only I know the secret of that."

And away went uTshwebe, walking over the lake until she disappeared behind some rushes, her chuckles coming back to the astonished monkey. Actually, the bird was not walking on the water at all. During the night the Great God had made uTshwebe's toes very,

very long, enabling her to walk on the water-lily leaves
in such a way that her weight was spread over the whole
leaf, which then sank about two centimetres below the
surface. To anyone watching, it appeared that the bird
was walking upon the water.

uTshwebe, the Jacana bird, still spends most of her
days trotting across the water-lily leaves but never, since
that day so long ago, has Monkey tried to jump at her
and steal some more of her feathers.

OBE And Helmet

HAD I not found myself in London with a few hours to spare before the train left that would take me home to Oxfordshire, I would never have dropped in at the Club and seen the obituary notice in *The Times*. These days my interests do not extend beyond the County news, as related in the local newspapers.

It was a very short notice. Only a couple of lines, in fact:

'The death has occurred in the Mzamuma Mission Hospital of Chief Marikari, OBE, of the Mngwara tribe. Chief Marikari received his OBE in 1945 for services to the Crown.'

That was all.

It was only to be expected, I suppose. Since his country had been granted independence, a young, ambitious man had come to power. Tribalism had been ruthlessly suppressed. Chief Marikari had faded quietly into obscurity.

Things had been very different when I was Governor General of the country. Marikari had assisted me in putting down a determined uprising planned by some of the young hotheads in the Mngwara tribe.

For this he had received the OBE, on my recommendation. Had I known of the events that would follow upon the investiture, I would have decided upon another form of reward for Marikari . . . But I might as well tell the story from the beginning.

Marikari was one of the few remaining Chiefs in the country who was a true traditionalist. At home in his great kraal he lived in primitive splendour, as the Chiefs of his tribe had for generations past. Not for him the European garb, or the Western way of life.

His six foot three inch, three-hundred-pound body would be draped with a leopard skin, a symbol of his status. Monkey skins and feathers completed the ensemble.

He made a truly impressive sight seated upon a throne of lion skins, surrounded by the courtiers of his household. A fan of dyed ostrich feathers wielded by a servant provided a source of cool air and kept pernicious flies away from the royal personage.

That is how I always saw him. It was how he received me when I called on him to give Marikari official notification of the honour that had been bestowed upon him It was an official visit. Unlike Marikari, I was overdressed in the formal attire of Governor General. With a high-necked collar buttoned beneath my chin, I was soaked with perspiration as I stood before him.

He nodded gravely but silently when the *Gazette* notice was read aloud for his benefit. Had I not been well acquainted with him, I would never have known of the intense pride he felt.

"Congratulations, Marikari," I said when the official document had been read. "I am very happy indeed that your loyalty and leadership has been rewarded. Now, let us discuss arrangements for you to receive the award. If you wish, you may go to London and receive it from the King. However, should this be inconvenient, we will arrange a ceremony at my residence and I will present it to you. Which would you prefer?"

After thinking the matter over for a few minutes, Marikari said, "I will go to London if you agree to come with me."

I was taken aback. Not because he wished me to travel with him. I was due for some leave. Going to London was a probability anyway. No, it was his wish to go to London. Marikari had not left his native land since the day he was born. I could see a number of complications . . .

"Hmm! Hrmmph . . .! Of course, if that is really what you wish, Marikari, but it raises a number of problems. You will find London a very different place from your kraal. Another thing, the investiture will be held in November. It is a very cold month in England. Very cold indeed."

I looked at his bulging figure, glistening in the heat of the African sun. "The, er . . . 'clothes' you are wearing at the moment would be quite unsuitable for England. You will need to wear European-style clothing."

There was a growl of dissent from the chief and a heated argument ensued. It ended, eventually, with a compromise. He would wear European clothes, but with two additions. The first was the Chief's badge. This was a highly decorated piece of metal, weighing at least a pound and a half, suspended from his neck by a leopard's tail.

The second 'extra' was an ancient pith helmet.

The helmet had been presented to Marikari's father by the first representative of the Crown to arrive in the country. Marikari wore it on every State occasion.

I agreed to the inclusion of these two emblems of his authority and returned to my official residence to work out the arrangements for the journey.

An Indian tailor made all the clothes that Marikari would wear and I had no difficulty procuring the necessary travel documents.

The most pressing problem was to find a pair of shoes large enough to fit Marikari's huge feet. It appeared he required a pair somewhere in the region of a size fifteen. It was found to be impossible to purchase a pair of such proportions. They needed to be specially made for him.

On the day of his departure, the airport was crowded with tribesmen and women. Some had walked for distances of up to fifty miles in order to give their Chief a suitable send-off. There must have been at least two thousand of them. Their ululating and singing completely drowned the music of the local regimental band, mustered for the occasion.

As he reached the top of the aircraft steps, Marikari turned. Taking off his pith helmet, a battered, off-white specimen, he waved it in the air to acknowledge the salute of his people.

The gesture brought forth a full-throated roar and the band came to an abrupt and discordant halt.

Marikari thoroughly enjoyed the flight, especially a

visit to the flight deck. I had the uncomfortable feeling that he spent the greater part of the journey trying to work out how many cows he would need to pay in order to own a similar means of transport.

We were met at London Airport by a junior official of the Commonwealth. After posing for a couple of dis-interested photographers, we reached our hotel without incident.

I was booked into the next room to Marikari. When I looked in to see how he was settling in, I found him unpacking his suitcases. They had been purchased for him especially for the journey from my governmental account.

I looked at the paraphernalia he had deemed it necessary to carry with him, with dismay. There were a couple of high-smelling cow hides, which Marikari assured me were necessary to ensure a good night's sleep. He had also brought his leopard skin – and a huge knobkerrie.

In reply to my astonished question, Marikari drew himself up to his considerable height. He assured me that although he would attend the investiture and meet the King dressed as a European, he intended dressing as a Chief of his tribe in the sanctuary of his own room.

Without more ado, he stripped off the clothing I had bought for him and donned his leopard skin.

The effect upon the manager and a waiter who accom-panied him, carrying a tray of fruit and flowers to the room, was startling. They stopped dead in their tracks!

Marikari, who happened to have the knobkerrie in his hand at the time, advanced upon them with the innocent intention of examining the fruit. The waiter promptly deposited the tray on a side table and both men fled from the room

I dabbed my brow with a handkerchief and thought that November in England was not as cold as I remembered.

I determined to keep Marikari under close surveillance for the duration of his visit. I could well imagine the effect it was likely to have on anyone of a nervous disposition should they chance upon Marikari, dressed in tribal accoutrements and swinging his knobkerrie, prowling the hotel corridors.

Actually, my task did not prove to be as difficult as I feared. Marikari behaved himself very well. He spent most of his time looking out over the city through the window of his hotel room. Although he proved a major attraction when I took him on a sight-seeing tour of London, he behaved with a quiet dignity here too.

I fear his exemplary behaviour lulled me into a sense of false security.

* * *

At last, the day of the investiture arrived. I accompanied Marikari, immaculate in his tailored suit, to Buckingham Palace. There was no fear of losing him in the crowd there. The battered pith helmet towered above the heads of the others at the investiture, like a beacon on a flat shore.

After explaining the details of the ceremony to him, I placed him in line with the other recipients of similar awards and stood back to watch as the queue shuffled towards the sovereign.

I need have had no qualms about the ceremony.

Marikari was the perfect gentleman. He shook hands politely, received his medal and bowed his head low when the King said a few words to him.

A beaming smile upon his face, he turned around and walked towards me, his gait awkward in the size fifteen shoes.

After admiring the medal, I led him away. It was a fine, crisp day and the investiture was being held on the palace lawns.

Finally, I decided it was time Marikari and I left. I guided him to our waiting car. It was not until he was folding his huge bulk through the door in to the vehicle that I noticed something was missing.

"Marikari!" I gasped. "Where are your shoes?"

He looked sheepish. "They hurt me too much, those shoes. I took them off and left them in the bushes."

"Oh no!" I groaned. I had a brief moment of madness when I considered returning and searching for the missing footwear. However, the thought of crawling around on my hands and knees, explaining to the distinguished gathering that I was searching for a pair of size fifteen shoes, caused me to shudder. I dismissed the idea.

Instead, I berated Marikari all the way back to the hotel for being so inconsiderate as to lose the only pair of shoes he possessed. I pointed out that it would be quite unthinkable for a man in his position, wearing the ribbon of the OBE, to be seen in public with nothing on his feet. I added that shoes of such a size would no doubt be as difficult to obtain in London, as they had been in his home country.

Although Marikari said nothing in his defence, I knew he was deeply ashamed of his indiscretion. He was silent

131

for the rest of the evening. I began to feel sorry I had made such an issue of the affair. It would probably not be too difficult to obtain a new pair. I decided I would make some inquiries the next day.

I went to bed fairly early that night as I had some other business to attend to the following morning.

I was awakened by a loud pounding on my door. Startled, I sat up and switched on the bedside lamp. My watch told me it was three o'clock!

The banging continued. Calling out that I was coming, I swung myself out of bed. Pulling on a dressing-gown, I went to the door and opened it.

A large police sergeant stood in the corridor outside, looking at me fiercely through one eye. The other was swollen and discoloured.

"Are you Sir Harold Featherthwaite?" he queried.

"Yes," I replied, wondering why this battered minion of the law should call on me at this hour of the morning. "Can I help you?"

"Are you the man in charge of a big African? A Chief something-or-other? Who runs around in a leopard skin, carrying an offensive weapon in the form of a big club?"

My heart sank to the region of my bare feet, "Oh no. Not Chief Marikari?! Isn't he . . .? He should be . . .!" Words failed me. Tottering back inside the room, I sank down in a chair. "Tell me, Sergeant. What has he been doing?"

"Well, sir," said the sergeant, "he was discovered climbing over the wall of Buckingham Palace. When we tried to apprehend him, he violently resisted arrest. It took thirteen of us to overpower him and there's three of my men in hospital. They're not seriously hurt, fortunately, but it was some fight, I can assure you, sir." He fingered his injured eye gingerly.

"We got him down to the station," he went on, "and it was then I noticed he was wearing the OBE. Most surprising, I thought, under the circumstances. Anyway, we got through to someone from the Commonwealth Office and they suggested we tried you. So, here I am!"

I put my head in my hands and groaned. "Tell me, Sergeant," I managed to say, after a few minutes. "What are the charges against him?"

The sergeant took a notebook from his pocket and thumbed over the pages. "Well, sir, there are quite a few. Attempting to break into the grounds of Buckingham Palace; violently resisting arrest; carrying an offensive weapon at night – that's rather more serious than having it in the daytime," he explained, cheerfully. "Causing bodily harm to a number of policemen . . ." He closed the notebook and returned it to his pocket.

"However, sir, the Inspector feels there might be some perfectly good explanation. He says he doesn't wish to make an international incident out of this. He said if you would be so good as to accompany me to the police station, you might be able to sort something out between you."

"Thank you, Sergeant," I said. "Give me a few minutes to get dressed and I will accompany you."

The sergeant started to leave the room, but paused in the doorway. "Oh yes! The Inspector says will you bring some more clothes for this Chief whatever-his-name-is. His leopard skin got a bit torn in the fight."

When I was fully dressed, I went to Marikari's room

133

and scooped up his European clothes. Almost without thinking, I picked up his pith helmet too.

Chief Marikari was sitting quietly in a cell in the police station. Apart from his leopard skin, which was hanging in tatters about his waist, he looked surprisingly undamaged.

He did not seem unduly perturbed about anything and changed into the clothes I had brought for him without saying a word.

When he was dressed and the pith helmet settled firmly on his head, the sergeant took us to the inspector's office.

I had already guessed what lay behind Marikari's unorthodox return to the Palace. I felt I was largely to blame because of the severe slating I had given him over the loss of his shoes. I did my best to explain all this to the inspector. "So you see," I ended, lamely, "I am quite certain he intended nothing unlawful. He merely went to the Palace to collect his shoes."

The inspector bowed his head to look at the documents on his desk and also, I suspected, to hide a smile.

"Well, Sir Harold," he said, when he looked up again, "in view of your explanation, I will not proceed with any charges against Mr Marikari. I will also do my best to keep the news of this matter from the Press."

I breathed a huge sigh of relief. "Thank you, Inspector. I really am most grateful to you – and to your men. *Most* grateful."

The inspector smiled, "As for your other problem, I think we might be able to do something about that too. There's a small shop around the corner where they sell boots and shoes to policemen. I happen to know they stock a size fifteen. I'll have a pair collected first thing this morning and sent around to your hotel."

I beamed with delight, "Inspector, you have been more than helpful. I am very sorry for all the inconvenience to which you have been put. I would like to make a substantial donation to your Widows and Orphans box and I trust the men in hospital will all make rapid recoveries."

I began to hustle Marikari out of the police station, but he was not quite ready to go. Breaking away from me, he advanced upon the sergeant.

The sergeant put up his fists defensively, but Marikari was no longer in a fighting mood. Before anyone could prevent him, he had removed the policeman's helmet and exchanged it with his own battered pith helmet.

Turning to me, he said, "Tell this man he fights very well. I wish him to have the hat of a Chief. I, too, fight very well, and I wish to have his."

I tried to explain to him that he could not go around exchanging headgear with policemen, but Marikari was adamant.

When I explained the position to the inspector and the sergeant, they both grinned widely.

"Well," said the inspector, "it's certainly most irregular, but as it would appear to be some form of tribal custom, I don't think there is anything that can be done about it. I am quite sure the Chief's helmet will be quite an acquisition for the Police Club."

He looked at Marikari, "I certainly don't think we should argue about it, do you, Sergeant?"

The sergeant looked out of his good eye and shook his

head, "Not again, sir. Not when I have another helmet at home."

And that is how Marikari came to be wearing a Metropolitan Police helmet when he stepped from the aircraft upon his arrival home.

It aroused a great deal of interest, of course, but I had made Marikari promise he would never tell anyone how he had come by it. Despite considerable pressure from the Press, I, too, have maintained a discreet silence on the subject.

I looked again at the obituary notice. I discovered that while I had been thinking of the past, I had picked up a pen that was kept beside the visitors' book.

After the letters OBE in the obituary, I had written, 'and Helmet'.

Render Unto Caesar

LEANING back against the grey police Land Rover, Police Superintendent Frederick Maple removed the pith helmet from his head and wiped the perspiration from his forehead with the back of a hand.

From the bush-veldt about him there was the multi-toned drone of insect life. Farther away, out of sight among the rocks on the hillside, a troop of baboons barked excitedly. A deep-chested young male had decided the time had come to challenge the authority of the grizzled old troop leader.

"Are you quite certain of the location of this village, Mutepfa? This track looks as though it has not been used for years." Superintendent Maple spoke loudly in a native dialect, looking over his shoulder.

"Oh yes, sir." Sergeant Mutepfa replied in the same language. Indeed, he found it difficult to follow a conversation in English. This was the reason he had spent most of his police career relegated to a country district.

Buttoning the front of his khaki shorts, he emerged from the long grass beside the track, "It is as I told you, sir. The headman of this village has paid no taxes for many, many years. In fact, until I spoke with the stranger

137

who was brought to my police station two months ago, it was not known the village existed. The people who live there do not like to come down from the hills and mix with other people. I knew you would want to see them, sir. To tell them they owe their loyalty to the government who looks after them, and to inform them they must pay their taxes, as the other villages do."

Frederick Maple felt there was a certain lack of logic in Sergeant Mutepfa's statement, but he had no desire to dispute the matter. It was too hot for argument. He was wishing he had not offered to make this tax collecting journey to the more remote areas of his district.

Usually such tax collections would be made by an inspector. Unfortunately, the man was on leave in England. His relief was down with malaria and the only other available officer had been married for only a few days. Superintendent Maple had rashly declared the trip would do him good. He would undertake it himself.

It had been so long since he had last been on patrol he had forgotten about the unbearable heat. It caused perspiration to ooze from every pore and his uniform stuck to his body like so many damp rags.

He had also forgotten the flies and mosquitoes which descended in a stinging cloud when he stepped from the vehicle; the smoky taste of tea brewed over a wood fire; the threatening presence of animals prowling around a night camp. There was one more thing he had almost forgotten. He remembered it now.

"Mutepfa! Will we be able to complete the journey in the Land Rover?"

"No, sir. Perhaps another ten miles only. Then we

have a four hour walk. If we start now we can arrive by
two o'clock, collect the taxes, and be back at the Land
Rover before dark. It will be better if we do not have
to stay in their village for the night."

Frederick Maple groaned his misery. A four hour walk
– and then four hours back again! For the last ten years
he had walked no farther than from his house, or the
police headquarters, to his car. The muscles of his legs
knotted at the thought of what was to come.

"All right, if you've finished what you were doing,
we'll make a move. I want to be back at headquarters
by tomorrow night. Let's go." He climbed in the vehicle,
pressed the starter and engaged four-wheel drive. The
vehicle lurched forward and they bumped away along
the winding, climbing track that disappeared among the
dark, wooded hills ahead of them.

The track became gradually narrower and less distinct.
Eventually, it petered out altogether, between some tall,
balancing rocks.

"This is it, Mutepfa. Nothing for it now but to continue
on foot."

Switching off the engine, the superintendent climbed
down from the vehicle, locked the door and pocketed the
key. Inspecting the back door, he made quite certain the
heavy padlock fitted to it was securely fastened. Inside
was the box, bolted to the vehicle, that contained the tax
money for the whole district. It was not a great sum, but
it might be sufficient to tempt a dishonest villager.

Satisfied the vehicle was secure, Frederick Maple
shrugged his shoulders into the straps of a small
pack. When it had been adjusted to his satisfaction,
he motioned for Mutepfa to lead the way.

With a much larger pack on his own back, Mutepfa strode off. He also had a rifle slung over his left shoulder and a heavy, carved, walking-stick clutched in his right hand.

Mutepfa never went anywhere without his stick. It was known and feared by would-be tax dodgers throughout the length and breadth of the district.

Many village headmen thought out ingenious excuses for not paying their taxes. All had suffered from the stick. Ruefully rubbing bruised heads, they had watched the sergeant walk away from them with their money. Receipts clutched in their hands provided mute evidence of the success of his crude methods.

Mutepfa's estimate of the distance of the village proved to be somewhat pessimistic. They had been walking for less than three hours when the superintendent was relieved to see the ground levelling off about them.

Then they came to cultivated fields of rustling maize plants. Here and there, herds of goats or cattle showed the were approaching the village occupied by the hitherto unknown tribe.

They saw no children guarding the livestock, but this was only to be expected. Frederick Maple knew from past experience that the presence of the two policemen would be known long before they reached the village. Herd boys would have hurried ahead to warn the headman of their coming.

Soon they began to descend in to a shallow valley. Just ahead they could see the blue smoke of cooking fires. It curled in the air above a large group of neat, thatched mud huts.

At the entrance to the village, the superintendent and

Mutepfa stopped. Coming towards them along the path was a group of men. These were the elders of the village.

Leading the group was a very old man. Yet, despite his white hair and wispy beard, he carried himself erectly. He had the proud bearing of a man used to having his orders obeyed by those about him.

What fascinated the superintendent was the dress of the village elders. They were all dressed alike in a garment that closely resembled a monk's habit, although the rough spun cloth was dyed in a wide variety of colours.

When the white haired man came to within a few feet of the superintendent, he stopped. Extending a hand to him, he said, in perfect English, "How do you do? It is not often we have strangers in our village. Still less often that the strangers are policemen."

It was with great difficulty that Superintendent Maple concealed his astonishment. Taking the proferred hand, he said, "Good day to you. I am astounded to hear you speak my language so well."

The headman smiled, "It is not really so surprising. We had a very good teacher, here in our village. His name was Brother Paul. He lived among us for very many years until he died, a much older man than I, only two years ago."

During these exchanges, Mutepfa, unable to follow what was being said, looked uncertainly from the headman to his superintendent. He was not sure whether or not to take a part in the conversation. As there did not appear to be any misunderstanding between them, he remained silent.

"I have a long and tiring journey back to my

headquarters," said Frederick Maple, "so I will get straight down to business. It has come to my attention that your village has not paid taxes for many years. In fact, I can find no record of you *ever* having paid them. As that appears to be due to an oversight on the part of the authorities, I am prepared to forget past taxes. However, under the laws of the country, everyone is required to pay a share towards the upkeep of the country's, er . . . facilities. I am here to collect your dues for this year."

The headman thought about the superintendent's words for a few moments. When he replied, his voice was quiet and thoughtful.

"I have heard about these taxes. They are paid by people who live far from here and who receive many things in return for the payments they make. We require nothing from anyone. Nor do we have anything we wish to give to them. Here in the hills we have always lived our lives in the way that is best for us. Why then should we pay taxes?"

This was a difficult question, but Superintendent Maple thought he had the right answer.

"I agree there may be nothing you require directly from the government, but the man in charge of the country is father to *all* his people. It is he who ensures you are allowed to enjoy your life in peace. He prevents others from crossing the borders of our country and interfering with your life. In order to do this he must have money to pay for the policemen and the soldiers; their uniforms and their guns. All this costs much money. It is for this reason you are required to pay taxes."

If the superintendent thought his argument would

142

persuade the other man to pay his taxes on the spot, he was mistaken.

The headman nodded his head wisely, "I understand the meaning of your words, but I do not agree with them. Brother Paul was a man of wisdom and peace. Many times he told us it is wrong to fight. Do not interfere with others and they will leave you alone, those were his words. They are true ones. We have not fought a battle since my father's time and others have not sought to fight with us. We have peace here. Why should we pay for those who do not think as we do? Who might use our money to fight with men we do not even know?"

Frederick Maple was slow to think of a suitable reply and the headman followed up his advantage.

"Look around you. What do you see? Our cattle are fat and contented. The crops grow well and feed my people. They are happy and peaceful. This is because Brother Paul taught us about the true God. We worship him in the manner he showed us."

The headman threw out his arms in an expansive, dramatic gesture. "It is to God we owe this, our prosperity. It is to God we pay our taxes."

It was the headman's sense of the dramatic that proved his undoing.

Mutepfa had become increasingly agitated at the tone of the headman's loud and authoritative voice. He had been straining his knowledge of English to the utmost in an attempt to follow the conversation.

The headman's final outburst was similar to many that Mutepfa had heard before. At last he believed he understood what was going on. Before the superintendent could make a move to prevent him, Mutepfa leaped forward and brought his stick down with a painful crack on the head of the village leader.

"You lie! It is a tale I have heard too many times from men like you. You say you have paid your taxes? Then show the superintendent your receipts."

Despite heat, flies and prowling animals, Superintendent Frederick Maple would not have missed that tax collection patrol for a year's pay.

He is retired now, but at every police reunion he can be heard retelling the same story. Of the day when Sergeant Mutepfa struck the headman of that remote village with his stick and demanded receipts for the taxes he had paid to God.

Ngauzani's New Coat

THIS is a tale of Ngauzani, the heron – the unhappy one. He has been unhappy for very many years, ever since that time, almost before memory, when all the birds were the same colour.

What that colour was has long since been forgotten, but it was a very ordinary colour and the birds were quite dissatisfied with it. As was their way, they held a meeting to discuss the matter.

"It really is rather awful," they agreed. "All around us are the trees and grasses looking most attractive with their various shades of green and brown, and we have to make do with this depressing plumage. What can we do about it?"

It was the weaver-bird who provided the answer. "I will tell you," he said. "In the beginning, I was given the magic for just this occasion. It was told to me that when you decided you would like to be more colourful I should weave new coats for you, and the colour I used for the coats would be yours for all time."

The birds were very excited. "This is wonderful," they cried. "But tell us, what colours will you use?"

"That has also been provided for," replied the weaver-bird. "I will have one whole day in which to make these

145

coats and I can use any colour that is to be seen on that particular day. It is for you to decide when it shall be."

There was much discussion on the subject. Some favoured the autumn when the leaves were shaded with soft browns and reds. Others preferred the warm yellows of summer. But the majority wanted it to be in the spring.

"That must be the time," they argued. "Think of all the colours to be seen. The wonderful, fresh green of the new grass peeping through the earth, and the flowers and the blossom on the trees. Yes, it must be in the spring, that is the finest time of all."

And so it was decided. They chose a particular day in spring and the weaver-bird made a careful note of it.

"But remember," he said, "you must not bother me while I am making these new coats. I have only been given so much magic and I must make them as quickly as possible with no time for idle chatter. They will all be thrown onto one big pile and you must choose for yourself the one you want. There can be no changing your mind once you have put it on."

The birds agreed and went away, chattering happily. But there was one bird who had not been at the meeting. This was Ngauzani. He was an extremely lazy bird and so he had decided that he would not bother to attend a dreary old meeting. Instead, he took a stroll by the river, hoping to find a fish or two for his lunch.

When he heard about the new coats they were to receive he merely shrugged his shoulders and yawned – and did not listen very carefully. When the day arrived he would go along and pick a coat for himself, he had no doubt there would be sufficient to go around.

As the great day approached the excitement of the birds reached fever pitch and there were very few of them who could sleep on that final night – but they made quite sure that nobody disturbed the weaver-bird.

The minute the sun showed his first edge above the horizon they made such a noise that the weaver-bird jumped from his nest and set to work. Never had he weaved quite so fast and, despite their promise, the others could not resist crying out in delight and pointing out each new colour to the busy little bird.

They found every imaginable colour. The rosy-pink of dawn, the clear blue of the sky and the darker blue of the silent pools in the river. Pure, white, fleecy clouds, the black shadows of the caves in the hills, flowers, trees, grass, all contributed to the colours of their new coats. Throughout the day the weaver-bird worked until, from the magnificent sunset, he took the reds, orange and purples that blazed in the sky.

By now he was quite exhausted and pausing only to take a bit of yellow from here and a touch of brown from there for his own coat, he hopped wearily away to his nest and tumbling inside fell fast asleep.

Now, Ngauzani had completely forgotten what day this was and had slept until very, very late. He then decided that he did not feel like doing very much and so he had sat on the river bank, dozing in the warm sunshine.

When the sun went down and it became a little chillier he thought he would take a walk. Soon he became aware of all the other birds laughing and talking among themselves and he went to see what was happening.

When he saw their most attractive new coats he became quite upset. "But why did nobody tell me that we were to receive our new coats today?"

"Oh Ngauzani!" the birds said, crossly. "We did tell you and, anyway, we have talked of nothing else for months now."

"Well, I don't really care," said the lazy heron, carelessly. "I will just have to get my coat tomorrow, that's all."

"Don't be silly," said all the birds together. "Weaver-bird only had the magic for one full day, tomorrow will be too late."

Ngauzani was quite alarmed. He HAD to have a new coat. He could not go through life wearing the dowdy one he had while all the others looked so beautiful. He hurried away to where the weaver-bird was sleeping in his nest and tried to wake him, but it was quite impossible. The little bird had worked so hard that he just could not be roused.

Ngauzani tried everything. He shook the nest until it nearly fell from the tree, he banged pieces of wood together and he shouted until he was almost hoarse, but all to no avail – the weaver-bird would not wake up. All night long the heron kept up his efforts until, faint in the East, he saw the pale light creeping into the sky. He was very close to tears now but he made a final effort and at last the weaver-bird showed some signs of stirring.

"Yes, what is it?" he said, opening one eye. "Who is that making so much noise?"

"It is me, Ngauzani. Please Weaver-bird, wake up. I

did not get a new coat yesterday. Please make one for me now."

"Really, Ngauzani!" said the weaver-bird, thoroughly angry. "You are such a lazy bird that you don't deserve a new coat and I am not at all sure that there is any magic left. Is the sun up yet?"

"No," replied the heron, "not quite."

"Humph!" said the weaver-bird. "Well, I might just have time, but the magic will disappear the minute the sun comes into the sky."

He jumped out of his nest knowing that he had to be very quick, but during the night the rain clouds had gathered and the only colour to be found was grey. There was dark grey and light grey and an even lighter grey but that was all and so these were all he could use for Ngauzani's coat.

The heron has never forgotten that occasion and you can see him today, standing on the bank of a river or a lake, hunched up, and unhappy.

As miserable as that dull, grey dawn, so long, long ago.

Come Unto Me

THE beautiful sound of music from the organ swelled beneath the tall arches of the ancient church. The morning sunlight, streaming in rainbow hues through the stained glass of fifteenth-century windows made magic of minute particles of dust, floating high above the altar.

The voices of the choir singing the morning hymn echoed from stout stone walls. Hilary Parfitt closed her eyes and clasped her hands in prayer, a wonderful sense of belonging stealing over her.

Hilary's imagination took her back over the hundreds of years of worship which had helped to mellow this place. She thought of all those who had found their peace here. Once there had been monks in cowl and robe, with serious faces and crossed hands. Peasants in simple smocks and gaiters. The nobles of the area, resplendent in satin and velvet . . .

Opening her eyes, she glanced at the congregation about her. There were elderly faces, intense and devout. And there were the young children. Fidgeting uncomfortably on the hard pews, they stared with uninhibited curiosity at the stone faces of cherubs and angels, carved around the tops of the huge, round pillars.

There was a fair sprinkling of teenagers too, she noted, with satisfaction.

It had been many years since Hilary was last in an English church. Years during which much had happened in her life.

There had been many memorable moments. Especially at the end of the day, when the last African had left the clinic in the particularly remote part of Africa where she had worked.

When this moment came she would wipe the perspiration from her brow and look out across the sun-parched land, longing for the quiet and cool of an English church.

Now she had returned to the country of her birth.

The sum total of those many years of dedication was a signed letter from the president of the country. He expressed the grateful thanks of his people for the untiring work she had performed for them.

And, of course, there was Tom.

Tom had been the clinic's doctor. With his quiet and efficient manner he had quickly gained the confidence of a suspicious people. In the small clinic he would treat anything from a festering splinter, to a wind-pipe torn by a wounded leopard.

Defying prejudice and taboo, custom and plain honest fear, he had given a new lease of life to people who fought a daily battle with disease and poverty.

Tom had never spared himself in his work. In the end, the rigours of a life far removed from civilisation, coupled with the primitive conditions in which he had to work, proved too much for him. He had held on for much longer than was good for him. He always hoped

151

another doctor would come along to take over his work. But he was to have no successor.

The truth was that although the troubles of the country had never touched him personally, the world regarded it as a land that was far too dangerous for a white man. Finally and unhappily, he had been forced by ill health to close the remote clinic. He left his life's work behind him, cut off at a time when he believed it to be most needed.

Hilary had accompanied him, her heart heavy within her. She knew he had only a short time to live.

Last night had been a particularly bad one. A high fever had racked Tom's body. It was the second such bout he had suffered in the month they had been back in England.

Not until the sun rose over the grey rooftops of the small Wiltshire town had he slept. It was a deep sleep and Hilary knew from hard-learned experience that he would not wake for many hours.

Suddenly she had heard the church bells ringing and remembered it was Sunday.

Her longing for the peace and tranquillity of an English church flooded back. Hurriedly tidying her hair, greyer than ever in the cruel morning light, she put on her coat. Quietly letting herself out of the door, she made her way to the church in the centre of the town.

It was a Communion service and the time had come for the congregation to stand while the vicar gave the appropriate exhortation. Then he called upon the congregation to come to the altar-rail to receive the wine and wafer that was representative of the body of Christ.

His voice droned on pleasantly and, drowsy from her

night's vigil, Hilary was not giving him her full attention. She was happy with her surroundings and the feeling of inner peace that it gave to her.

Perhaps this is why the dreadful words were spoken and past before she realised the full import of them.

For a minute she thought she had misheard. There *had* to be some mistake. Hastily she turned the pages of her prayer book, seeking the exhortation which the vicar was quoting.

Here it was. Hilary searched the closely written lines. Staring up at her from the yellowing pages, they seemed to grow in size. The words she had hoped she would not find.

The congregation was filing from the pews towards the altar-rail to receive the Sacrament, but Hilary was not with them. She pressed forward against the hard wood of the pew in front, allowing those in her row to reach the aisle.

When they had gone she sank to her knees, her mind in a turmoil. Her peace of mind shattered.

The soft murmur of the vicar's voice came to her as though from another world. Gradually, the congregation returned to their places.

She remembered very little of the remainder of the service. She was not even aware it had ended until the others started moving about her.

She waited until the last of them had gone. Then she, too, made her way to the church door.

The vicar was standing here, a smile on his face. He put out his hand to shake hers. Pretending not to see it, she made to walk past him, but he restrained her with a gentle touch on her arm.

"I have not seen you here before," he said, quietly. "I am always especially happy to welcome newcomers to our community. I noticed you did not take Communion. Are you in trouble? Perhaps there is some way in which I may be of assistance?"

She hesitated, momentarily uncertain. Then she looked at the vicar, his round, healthy face smiling at her in a kind, vague manner. Her mind conjured up another face. A face unshaven and ravaged with sickness. Gaunt with suffering. Brought about by his unselfishness and regard for his fellow men.

"No," she said, her mind made up. "No, there is nothing you can do. Thank you for your kind offer. Perhaps, when the appropriate time comes I will be able to put the facts of my situation before one who will understand."

Drawing on her gloves, she hurried away. To Tom. But the words of the prayer book remained a painful scar in her mind.

They were words she would never be able to forget:

'. . . Therefore, if any of you be a blasphemer of God, an hinderer or slanderer of His word, an ADULTERER, or be in malice, or envy, or in any other grievious crime, repent you of your sins, or else come not to that holy table . . .'

Perhaps things might have been different had Tom not been already married when Hilary met him. Married to a woman he had not seen for very many years. With whom he had spent only a brief period of his life – but a woman who refused to divorce him.

154

True, there would then have been no African clinic. No medical aid for desperate people. No life-saving medicine for otherwise doomed babies. No easing of pain for those who had no one else to care about them.

She wondered whether that would have mattered to the Established Church. After all, they were not *Christians*!

And at least Tom and Hilary would have been able to celebrate Holy Communion. Together, if the opportunity had arisen.

When Hilary reached the home she shared with Tom she carefully put the prayer book at the bottom of the trunk that contained the possessions she no longer used.

Tip-toeing quietly in to the room where Tom lay sleeping, she kissed him gently on his furrowed and sun-burned forehead.

The Chameleon

LONG, long ago, in the beginning of time, when man and the beasts were brothers and did not raise their hands, one against the other, the world was a wonderful place. Sweet water flowed from the hills, the earth was fertile and crops flourished. There was enough, and more, for everyone.

The Great God who had created the world dwelled high on the tall, sacred mountain where no man was allowed to set foot. He was well pleased with the result of his labours. Well pleased but for one thing.

Although fighting was unknown, arguing was not – and man had proved to be the most argumentative creature in the land! Whenever two men from different tribes met each other they would squat down on their haunches and proceed to argue which of their respective tribes was the better.

Even in the villages among their own people they would spend many hours in quarrelsome debate. Seeking to find the answer to the question of why this cow was brown and that one was black and white, or whether this wife or that one was the better cook.

Once, the men of one village sat cross-legged around the fire the whole of the night, until the stars in the velvet sky dimmed and faded into dawn, discussing where the flames from the fire had gone when only the dull, glowing charcoal was left.

The Great God would not have minded had the men been able to arrive at their own conclusions to each argument, but they could not, and each one ended in the same way. As man was forbidden to walk upon the sacred mountain they would send one of the animals to ask the Great God the answer.

It was not only the Great God who was annoyed with this state of affairs. The mountain was a long way from the villages of the tribes and its sides were very steep, with the result that at the end of the journey the animals were very weary. And so it came to pass that whenever an argument started all the animals would run away and hide in places where they could not be found.

This is what happened on the day of the last big discussion, when many tribes were gathered in one village. It was about sleep. Where, they said, does a man go when his body sleeps? They mentioned the dreams that come to a man during those dark hours. Is he living those things, or is he not?

Backwards and forwards went the words, now supporting this theory, now that one, and still they were no nearer to finding an answer. The animals, realising that this argument would end in the same manner as so many others, had long since found hiding places and when deadlock was reached and the men were calling out for a messenger to be sent to the Great God, none could be found.

The villagers searched everywhere for them, but without success. All they could find were a lizard and a chameleon, both of whom had been asleep on a rock, so contented with the sun's warmth that they had not even been aware of the argument.

The men would have preferred to have sent the fleet-footed buck, or even the sturdy, galloping zebra, both of whom would have brought them a speedy reply from the sacred mountain but, despite the grumbles of the more impatient ones among them, they realised that they had no alternative but to despatch the lizard and the chameleon.

It was late afternoon when the two set off on their journey. They were good friends and found much to talk about so that the journey, at first, was quite pleasant. Then, almost before they realised it, the sun disappeared over the horizon and it became quite dark.

They had never been on the sacred mountain before and in the darkness they strayed from the path and lost their way many times. Eventually, they arrived at the dwelling of the Great God in the early hours of the morning. Their stumbling in the darkness wakened him and he hurried out to meet them, wondering what had brought them to see him at this time of the night.

As they explained about the argument that the people wished him to resolve for them he became extremely angry. His eyes flashed forth lightning that reached out to the furthermost corners of the earth and the echo of his voice sent whole mountains tumbling, crashing into the valleys.

"So!" said the Great God. "So! Despite the many things I have given to them, food, water and peace on the face of the earth, yet still they are not happy. Still they continue with these silly arguments and quarrels about things that are of no consequence. Very well, they shall have their reply. In fact, they shall have two replies and whichever one reaches them first, then so shall it be from this time hence. There will be no turning from it. This is my word."

He turned to the chameleon. "You, Chameleon, shall take this answer. From this day, the mind of man shall be as the mind of God. All things shall be revealed to them. They shall have life eternal and, when they sleep, their dreams shall reveal to them more than they ever knew. When they awaken, the meanings of these dreams shall be clear. Their daily life shall remain as it is today, full of peace and plenty. That is your message to my people, Chameleon."

Then he spoke to the lizard, and once again the thunder and lightning went forth over the face of the earth.

"To you, Lizard, I give this message. The days of milk and honey are ended. No more will my people be provided with all that they require, they will have to seek and work for it. No more will they live in peace with their neighbours, and when they quarrel the result will be fighting and bloodshed. Their sleeping hours will be filled with dreams that have no answer until one day they sleep a sleep from which there shall be no awakening. Only on that final day, when life is ended, shall the answer to life be given to them."

He finished speaking, and looking first at the lizard and then at the chameleon he shook his head sadly. "Now you must return to those who sent you. I know that you are tired but you must go as fast as you are able. Whoever reaches the people first will decide their fate, because his message will decide the future of man, for ever and ever."

The lizard and the chameleon realised that he was indeed a very Great God, and without even a word to each other they set off on the return journey as fast as they were able. At first, on the downward slopes of the mountain, they travelled side by side but when they reached level ground the chameleon began to feel very, very tired and dropped behind.

Not so the lizard. He raced on as fast as his short legs would carry him, scuttling around trees and over rocks, through bushes and clumps of tall grass. Even when the sun came up, red and gold over the horizon, he did not pause or slacken his pace.

The chameleon moved slower and slower until you could scarcely see him moving. When the sun came up it dazzled him and he closed his eyelids until only the merest pin-prick of eye was to be seen. He was so tired that for long periods he appeared to be asleep on his feet, standing sometimes with one leg poised in the air. Only the tiny spot of eye that could be seen indicated that he was still awake.

All that day he travelled in this slow manner and night had fallen once again before he reached the village from which he had been sent. Going into the first hut he told the occupants his story but they laughed at him.

"Go away, Chameleon," one of them said. "Do not come to me with your lies. The lizard returned this morning and he had the answer to our question. Go and tell your stupid story to the people in the next village, they may be foolish enough to believe you – but you had better go quickly, tomorrow they will not be there. When the dawn comes we are going to fight them and will prove that we are better than they."

Slowly, the chameleon left the hut and made his weary way to the next village. Entering the hut of the headman he found him busily sharpening a spear. The headman was no more inclined to believe him than the others had been.

"Run away, Chameleon," he sneered. "I myself heard the words of the lizard this morning. Do not try to trick me. I believe you have been sent by the men from the other village. They are frightened because they realise that we will defeat them in battle tomorrow."

Sadly, the chameleon left that village also. He made his way to the next, and the next, and the next – but always the lizard had been before him.

But he never gave up.

Even today he may be seen, tired and slow, eyes squinting against the sun, making his way from village to village, hoping to find a place where the lizard has not yet been.

Habits Die Hard

CONSTABLE CHARUMA was overweight, cheerful – and thoroughly exasperating!

He stood before Inspector Alden, supposedly at attention, shifting from one foot to the other, the front edge of his khaki police tunic curving from one gleaming button to the next.

Adrian Alden flicked through the pages of the personal file lying open on the desk before him, passing from one misdemeanour to another.

When he had finished, he closed the file slowly and looked up at Charuma. The grin which put in an appearance on the African's face was hastily stifled as the Inspector frowned.

Standing up, Alden paced up and down behind his desk, his right hand slapping his leg in time with each precise step.

He was a slight, pinched-faced man with a bristling moustache and the bearing of a military man. It would have come as no surprise to anyone meeting him for the first time, to learn he had been a captain in the British Army before joining the Colonial Police.

Inspector Adrian Alden lived for his work, was a strict disciplinarian, and had very few close friends.

For a few minutes he paced backwards and forwards, his progress followed by Charuma's eyes. When he stopped, the desk was between the two men.

"Charuma!" The voice was as spiky as the moustache. "How many times have you appeared before me in this office and been warned about your future conduct? Once? Twice? Three times?"

Charuma smiled cheerfully, "Three times, boss. One time when I beat the man who said unkind things about the police. Another time when I fell asleep on duty because I had been to the wedding of my sister. Then there was the time that the boss has probably forgotten. I was very new at the station at the time. I awoke late and was too tired, boss. I paraded for duty but had forgotten to put my boots on."

Alden's face became very pink and he glowered at the cheerful African.

"Three times in twelve months!" The words came out as an explosion. "And how many times have you been told that you call your officers 'sir' and not 'boss'? You are supposed to be a policeman, not a houseboy!"

Picking up a ruler from the desk, Alden prodded Charuma in the place where he bulged most, between the second and fourth buttons of his tunic.

"Look at you! Your very shape makes it obvious to me what kind of a policeman you are. Fat, lazy – and thoroughly useless!"

He was getting warmed up now. Picking up the file he resumed his pacing, pausing to occasionally stab an incriminating finger in Charuma's direction.

"Three times you have appeared before me on disciplinary charges, not to mention the numerous lesser offences entered on your personal file. Dirty belt; absent from duty through sickness – that's another way of saying you were drunk; being insolent to your sergeants . . ."

He threw the file on the desk in disgust, "I have had enough of you, Charuma. I am not prepared to tolerate your conduct any longer. Discipline is absolutely essential in this force – but discipline is the very quality that is lacking in you.

"Very soon your duties would have taken you to the Northern border valley, fighting dissident tribesmen. If you lack the most elementary discipline and fail to do what you are told without question in a battle situation, you are a danger to yourself and to every man who is with you."

Inspector Alden suddenly stopped his pacing. Dropping down heavily in his chair, he scraped it noisily across the polished wooden floor as he drew it closer to the desk.

Taking a fountain pen from his breast pocket, he began writing in Charuma's personal file, talking to the African as he did so.

"I have no alternative but to dismiss you from the Service, Charuma. It will take effect from tomorrow. In the morning you will hand in your uniform and report to the pay office to collect whatever money is due to you. You will, of course, vacate your single quarters before nightfall tomorrow."

The smile faded from Charuma's face and was replaced by an expression of bewilderment.

164

"But . . . I like being a policeman, boss. It is a good job for me and it makes my father very proud."

Alden did not even look up, "That is something you should have thought of before. It's too late now. You may leave, Charuma."

"But I am a good policeman, boss. I have caught many bad men."

Inspector Alden put his pen down on the desk with a gesture of impatience, "Charuma, I have no intention of arguing with you. This interview is at an end. You have been dismissed. Now, get out of my office before I lose my temper. Out! OUT!"

The last two words were shouted and the movement of the inspector's hand practically brushed Charuma from the room.

With an expression on his face that showed he was still inclined to argue against the inspector's decision, Charuma edged out of the doorway.

Inspector Alden continued writing in Charuma's file for another ten minutes before replacing the pen in his pocket. Then he read through the report.

Satisfied, he inked his official stamp and brought it down heavily upon the file. Closing it, he dropped it into his 'Out' tray.

Taking his hat from the peg behind the door, Alden left his office and walked out of the building to his car.

He would be glad when he was out of this place. His request for a posting to the Special Service Unit had been approved. In another month he would be free from the paperwork that went with running a suburban police station and dealing with men like Charuma.

Entering the car, he turned the key, reversed it across the yard and drove out to the street beyond.

*   *   *

Inspector Alden soon settled into the routine of his new duties on the border. Being a bachelor, there was nothing to distract him. He devoted all his attention to the patrols and interceptions that were so much a part of police work in this part of the country.

There were reports of a big build-up of exiled tribesmen across the river. Intelligence bulletins were flooding in thick and fast. It became apparent that it was not a question of *whether* the rebels would cross, but when, and where.

The expected raid came shortly before dawn on a Sunday morning. Alden was awakened by his radio operator who had just received the message.

"A large party has crossed the river about five miles east of here, sir. Headquarters say we are to move off in that direction and make contact with them – but we are to shadow them only. It's estimated they are more than fifty strong. A company of the army is being sent to join forces with us. We are to take no action before they reach us."

As he dressed, Alden gave orders for the camp to be roused. He already had a number of patrols out. Unfortunately, all of them had been sent in directions away from the terrorists. He could muster no more than nine men.

The rising sun was shining directly into the eyes of his small force as it set out on foot. It was difficult terrain

166

and the path would soon became far too narrow for a vehicle. They were making for a point where Alden hoped they might intercept the tribesmen.

The position of the sun might have been responsible for no one in the patrol seeing the rebels, or it might have been that they had been given an incorrect map reading for the crossing. Whatever the cause, the small force was little more than a mile from its base camp when it was caught in an ambush and subjected to a heavy crossfire.

The siting of the ambush was perfect. The tribesmen were almost invisible on a small hill dotted with tumbled, broken rocks. The hill completely dominated the path along which the policemen had been walking.

Fortunately, the accuracy of rebel shooting was not of the best and none of the policemen were hurt in that initial burst of gunfire.

Alden reacted quickly, "Quick! Get back to those trees while I cover you." He pointed to a small copse, a short distance back along the path.

As the policemen sprinted off to obey his orders, he dropped to one knee and fired a short burst into the rocks on the hillside.

He fired two more bursts. Then, looking over his shoulder, he saw the last of his men reach the safety of the trees.

Alden turned to follow them. As he did so there was the harsh chatter of a light automatic weapon from the rebel-held rocks and it felt as if someone had hit him in the back with a large stone.

He fell forward onto his face. When he tried to rise from the ground he was unable to do so. His legs would not obey his brain, although he felt surprisingly little pain.

After a few attempts he did managed to roll on to his back and felt more comfortable in this position.

His men had opened fire from the trees now. He could hear the gunfire and distinguish between the weapons of his own men and those of the terrorists. However, when he tried to raise his head to see what was going on he found it would not respond. His brain was giving the necessary orders, but the paralysis that affected his legs appeared to be spreading. His muscles refused to react.

He felt vaguely as though he were lying in bed, half-listening to something that was happening on the radio.

But it was an uncomfortable bed. Not that his wound bothered him. Like the battle, it was less than real. Something that might have been inflicted upon someone else.

It was the small stones beneath his body that he found uncomfortable. One in particular was pressing in the back of his neck and he became very angry that he could do nothing to remove it.

He lost all awareness of time. He probably lost consciousness for a while. Certainly, when he looked upwards he was aware that the sun had crept higher in the sky. It was not yet right above him, but it was high enough to cause him to squint.

He was hot. The perspiration trickled down his face. With the tip of his tongue he could taste the saltiness of it at the corners of his mouth.

His breathing was laboured and heavy now. His chest seemed to be rising more than twice its normal distance before falling to depths it had never known before.

Suddenly, he realised the noise of battle had intensified. He could hear the sound of a mortar being fired. It meant only one thing. The army had arrived!

There was another sound nearer at hand. The sliding, slithering noise of someone making a cautious approach on their stomach. He could not make out the direction from which it was coming. It might be friend – or foe.

Then he felt a touch on his arm. A moment later a round face, glistening with perspiration loomed above him – but it was the grin he recognised immediately.

"Charuma!" His voice came out harsh, cracked, and jerky, like a shunted train. "W-what . . . are you . . . doing here?"

"Shh! Don't try to speak, boss. I am a soldier now. I have come for you."

While he spoke, Charuma's hands were feeling beneath the inspector's body, trying to locate the wounds.

When he pulled them away they were red with blood. Just then a burst of firing from the terrorists' position sliced through the grass, only a few feet away.

"Charuma, go!" Alden gasped out. "I'm . . . dying. Leave me."

"A man should die with his own people. Not alone, staring at the sky, boss."

Kneeling beside Alden, seemingly oblivious of the shooting, Charuma lifted the helpless inspector in his arms. Then he was running with him.

For a moment the battle flared into a frenzy as the tribesmen tried to bring down Charuma, and the army and police gave him covering fire.

For the first time since he was shot, Alden felt pain. Agonising, scream-making pain as Charuma ran with him. Then the African soldier stumbled to the safety of the trees and waiting hands took his burden from him.

The battle lasted another half an hour before the mortars won the day. The surviving tribesmen abandoned the small hill and retreated to the border.

A doctor was accompanying the army. He did all that was possible for the inspector. Now Alden lay on a stretcher in a small tent, awaiting a helicopter that would take him to hospital. The doctor told the commanding officer that it was doubtful if he would live long enough to see it arrive.

Charuma lifted the flap of the tent and made his way slowly and quietly to the inspector's side.

Conscious, but heavily sedated, Alden looked up at the soldier, his mouth trying to form words. When they came they were so soft that the African had to bend low to hear them.

Straightening up, Charuma fumbled with the front of his tunic, his gaze never leaving the face of the inspector.

Alden began gasping for breath. Entering the tent hurriedly, the doctor pushed Charuma to one side and reached for the oxygen cylinder. Before he could operate it, the policeman gave a terrible shudder, then lay still.

Inspector Adrian Alden was dead.

Charuma walked slowly to where the men of his regiment were seated on the ground. For once a smile was absent from his round face.

"The Nkosi is dead," Charuma said, in answer to his sergeant-major's question.

"That is sad," said the sergeant-major, shaking his head. "He was a brave man. Did he speak to you before he died?"

"Yes." Charuma avoided the eyes of the other man and stared out across the wide river valley. "He told me to do up the top button of my tunic."

Nyati

FOLLOWING in the wake of the main herd, his nostrils caked with the dust kicked up by five hundred other buffaloes, old Nyati sneezed and plodded slowly onward.

His legs were stiff with advancing years, yet it was not this that caused him to lag behind the others. His isolation was the outcome of his battle with the younger bull, that morning. The head-jarring, side-slashing fight that had deposed him from his long-held position as leader of the herd.

In full view of the huge, silent, watching animals, he had been forced to his knees. An acknowledgement of the younger, stronger buffalo's superiority.

It made no difference that he had been a fine leader, fighting for their survival through so many changing seasons. There was no word for loyalty in the unwritten book of the wild. Strength was all.

The fight over, the herd turned from him, to follow their new leader. Nyati was left standing alone, his sides heaving. Blood from his wounds congealing in the heat of the African sun. Deserted, save for the busy, stinging flies that swarmed in dense black masses about his wounds.

Angrily he swung his head, the long red tongue

sweeping the stinging insects away. They rose in a small black cloud, only to settle once more within seconds.

The outcome of the contest might have been different had it taken place later in the day. When the chills of night were not still fresh in his joints. But it was too late now. The battle had been fought, and he had lost.

He knew what the future held for him. For a few days he would remain on the fringe of the herd, a target for the younger bulls whenever he ventured too near them. Then, gradually, they would accept him back. An anonymous buffalo in the herd, he would stay with them until the morning came when he was too feeble to rise.

They would go on their way without him. There would be no gap in the herd to mark his absence. He would already have been forgotten by the other animals. Only the gathering ring of circling, greedy vultures above, and slavering, ill-tempered, evil-smelling hyenas below would pinpoint the spot where he lay.

It was late afternoon now. In the lengthening shadows, the great herd approached the waterhole.

This was the time when leadership counted. The most dangerous time in any animal's day.

In spite of his inexperience, the young bull was cautious. Nyati watched him advance slowly. Very slowly. Head down and nose advanced, his nostrils flared as he sought the smell that would mean trouble. Lion trouble.

The great span of his heavy horns swept around as he breathed the air first one way, and then the other. Two paces forward and the procedure was repeated.

Another two paces.

The impatient herd piled up behind him, those in

the lead being forced forward by the sheer weight of numbers coming along behind them.

As Nyati watched, some of the calves were forced from the herd by the ever-increasing pressure.

This was the young leader's first mistake. Nyati looked on as the calves wandered further from the milling animals, seeking refuge from the choking dust.

When Nyati was leading the herd, he always ensured the younger animals remained closely bunched together. One stentorian bellow had been sufficient to send the calves scurrying back to safety.

Any order he gave now would go unheeded. Yet the years of leadership could not be forgotten in a single day. He remained as alert as he had always been.

The bulk of the herd was becoming impatient now as the new leader stopped again, uncertainly. Something was not as it should be. Neither the eyes nor the nose could find anything wrong, yet instinct was troubled.

As he stood, unsure of what he should do next, the adult buffaloes strained forward, awaiting the signal to drink. Meanwhile, Nyati continued to watch the calves.

Two, in particular, held his attention. They were young bulls. In growing apprehension he watched their hornless duel. Heads down and tails up, they charged each other, their game taking them farther and farther from the herd. Soon they were close to the long grass, standing tall and golden-dry beyond the mud of the waterhole.

Suddenly, Nyati saw the movement he had been half-expecting: not twenty paces from the mock battle of the calves, the grass trembled for a moment, then was still.

174

Nyati

There was not the faintest breath of a breeze to cause such a movement. To his experienced eye it meant only one thing: Lion!

Perfectly camouflaged, tail twitching and golden eyes gleaming, it would be working its way silently forward. Then would come the powerful lunge, spelling death for an unsuspecting calf.

This should have been seen by the new leader. It was a leader's duty – but this was no time for futile recriminations.

Slowly at first, but rapidly gathering speed, Nyati charged. Hooves pounding the ground, his huge old body swept forward with the inevitability of an express train.

Behind him, the other buffaloes snorted in alarm.

The sight of their late leader bearing down upon them at speed terrified the young calves. Ceasing their play, they bleated with alarm as they cleared his path and ran for the shelter of the herd.

Moments later, the angry roar of a thwarted lioness added to their terror.

She was hungry. The sight of her meal rapidly disappearing was more than she could accept. She broke from cover, her thin, tawny body stretched in pursuit of the nearest calf.

In her desperation she came too close to the old bull. He swerved to meet her and the two animals came together in a snarling, bellowing, dust-filled tangle that sent the herd stampeding towards the horizon.

The ferocious death-fight had no witnesses. No eyes of either human or beast saw the violent slashing of those terrible claws, or the throat-ripping savagery of yellow teeth.

175

There was no one to observe the dying efforts of the old bull, Nyati. On his knees, he shook his head wearily in a futile last attempt to free the lioness impaled upon one of his curving horns.

It was all over before the blanket of dust raised by two thousand hooves fell gently back to earth to settle on the two still bodies.

By the time the buffalo herd wearily picked its way back to the waterhole there was little to show for the self-sacrifice of Nyati.

Nothing but the slinking form of a jackal, bearing a bone away to the privacy of its lair.

That and a grotesque, bloated vulture. Awkwardly, it hopped along the ground, the great wings spread until the ungainly body was lifted into the air.

Soaring up towards the setting sun, the bird cast a long shadow over the waterhole.

Another African day was almost at an end.

The Season Of Life

THE old man sat cross-legged on the hard, dry earth in the doorway of his hut, looking out over the vastness of Africa.

Close to the village were rocky outcrops of rock. Giant boulders balancing precariously one upon the other. Beyond them, for as far as could be seen, were the hills. They dipped and soared until they fused into a purple haze in the far distance.

This was Chigavara's land. His home – and he loved it.

True, the colours were no longer as bright to his smoke-reddened old eyes. Nor was the difference between light and shadow as clearly defined as it had been in his younger days. But it mattered little. The scene before him was etched upon his heart. He did not need to see it.

Winter was drawing to a close now, the bush-veldt a mixture of dull browns and yellows. Many of the trees were still bare and, in the mornings, it still took a long time for warmth and feeling to return to Chigavara's limbs.

He sat now, drawing contentedly on his pipe – and thinking. He had long ago realised that life and the seasons were very similar. First, there was Spring. The beginning. When life was fresh and new and experiences opened out gently, like blossoms on a tree. A time of gradual awakening.

Then came Summer. A time of heat and passion. An African summer. Harsh and cruel. When the fruit of the plant that had been sown in the spring showed itself full and ripe – unless it had been touched with disease.

All too soon, the summer came to an end, to merge, almost unnoticed, with Autumn.

"And this," mused Chigavara, "is surely the most difficult time of all. An in-between time. When Summer is still close and reluctant to depart. When, on a good day it is easy to believe that it is still the hot season."

But such days gradually became less frequent. Eventually, one was forced to concede that Winter had truly arrived.

Winter had come long ago for the old man. So long, that it sometimes seemed to him that his Autumn, Summer and Spring had happened to someone else. Seasons he had seen, but in which he had taken no part.

He coughed and spat, wrinkling his nose and running his tongue over his lips. The pipe in his mouth had gone out while he was thinking. He had sucked in dry, bitter ash.

With shaking hands, he removed the pipe from his mouth and placed it upon the ground beside him.

From the path which followed the course of the river, he heard the unmusical sound of a bicycle bell. It was insistent and jarring to his ears and brought an immediate response from the young children in nearby huts. They began pleading and cajoling for coins.

There were disappointed wails from those whose demands were not met; shouts of delight from the others. The lucky ones rushed down the slope towards the river, money clutched in dark little hands. A few minutes later they returned, sucking noisily at coloured ice on a stick.

Chigavara winced at the sight of them. Once, someone had bought one for him. He still recalled the pain he had experienced in his few remaining teeth, when the ice had touched raw nerves.

As a child he had never known such luxuries as ice creams. In those days he rarely ever saw the village in daylight, unless it was from a distance. At dawn, he and the other children would be out with the cattle.

They would not return until the sun had disappeared behind the hills, its fiery after-glow lighting their way. The cosy smell of woodsmoke from the fires, and the aroma from the cooking-pots greeted them as they approached the village. It speeded their efforts to secure their charges and take their places around cooking-fires for the evening meal.

Another sound came to disturb Chigavara's thoughts of the long ago. A young man wearing European clothing walked past the hut. He was swinging a transistor radio from his hand. The speaker spewed forth the noisy, jerky music that the old man disliked so much.

He followed the young man with his eyes and shook his head. That one lived in the white man's city, doing a woman's work in the houses there.

179

With an effort, he thought back to the first time he had ever seen a white man. It was long ago, when the Spring of his life was almost Summer.

They had come into his country mounted on horses – but they had dismounted to fight.

Chigavara had been in the second rank of the warriors sent to oppose them. His shield over his arm, the blade of his assegai flashed bright and unblooded before his face.

Aaii! But that had been a day for men! When it was over, the blade of his assegai was no longer gleaming. Instead, it had been dull and bloody.

He recalled that he had stood for a long time looking down at the bodies of the white men. There were not more than could be counted upon the fingers of three men.

Yet all around them lay the dead warriors of his tribe. They were as plentiful as the droppings of a great herd of buffalo.

When the warriors left the battlefield, they had saluted the bravery of the slain white men. A booming shout that burst forth from a thousand throats. A thousand spears held high in the air. The ground trembling from the thud of stamping feet.

That had been music to his ears, not this discordant sound, like the wailing of women, that came from a small box.

Slowly, painfully, Chigavara rose to his feet. His frail body bent low, he made his way to the fire that had burned down to glowing ashes in the centre of the hut.

180

Lighting a twig, he held it to the bowl of his pipe, coughing a little as he sucked acrid smoke into his lungs.

He was indeed well into the winter of his life. Even the trivial act of rising to his feet tired him. He would lie down and rest for a while. Soon it would be time for Chikwinu and Amende to return from the fields and prepare the evening meal.

He smiled at the thought of Chikwinu. Now there was the fruit of his summer. Not his son, but his grandson. A fine boy who respected his grandfather. Who was genuinely pleased to do the many little things that helped to make an old man's life more bearable.

And Amende, Chikwinu's wife. Heavy with child now, she was still able, and willing, to carry out her full share of the work. Yes, he had sown his seed well.

He eased himself down on the blanket, laid out in the corner of the hut. He would lie here and smoke for a while. Then he might close his eyes and sleep for a short while.

That is how Chikwinu found him when he returned from the fields.

The pipe bowl was still warm. Warmer than the lifeless hand that held it. The old man's face was relaxed in a smile. His passing had been easy.

The numbers of Chigavara's family were not depleted for long. A son was born to Amende that very night. A strong, lusty child whose voice awakened the occupants of the adjoining huts as the dawn glimmered pink and grey in the sky.

As the sun came up, flooding the land with its golden

light, it could be seen that the first buds were bursting forth on the trees and bushes.

Another spring had arrived, and the baby would be named . . . Chigavara.